# Work, Rest and Play
# ACCORDING
# to ALEX

Kathryn Lamb lives 'quietly' in Gillingham, Dorset, with her six children and five cats. Without the help of her family she would have found it a lot more difficult to write this book.

She would like to thank them all, including some very special grandparents. Kathryn draws cartoons for *Private Eye* and *The Oldie*. She has written and illustrated a number of books for Piccadilly Press, which have been published in many languages throughout the world (including Italian, German, Dutch, Thai, Russian and Korean!).

# Work, Rest and Play
# ACCORDING
# to ALEX

## Kathryn Lamb

PICCADILLY PRESS • LONDON

First published in Great Britain in 2002
by Piccadilly Press Ltd.,
5 Castle Road, London NW1 8PR

Text, illustrations and cover illustration
copyright © Kathryn Lamb, 2002

The right of Kathryn Lamb to be identified as Author and
Illustrator of this work has been asserted by her in accordance with
the Copyright, Designs and Patents Act 1988

A catalogue record for this book is available from
the British Library

ISBN: 1 85340 712 7 (trade paperback)

1 3 5 7 9 10 8 6 4 2

Printed and bound in Great Britain by Bookmarque Ltd

Design by Judith Robertson

Set in 10.5pt Palatino and 14pt Soupbone bold

## Tuesday June 25th

**NEW ME!**

Rejoice!!! Ring out wild and CRAZEEE bells!!! In less than a week's time I will be let loose on an unsuspecting world for my Work Experience. No more school for two GLORIOUS weeks! Cry FREEEEEDOM!!! So look out World – here I come AND SO DO MY FRIENDS . . .

## Friends

**ABBY**

**Abby:** UNDOUBTEDLY my Best Friend DESPITE the STRANGE and WORRYING choice she has made for her Work Experience (see below).

**Age:** 16

**Chosen Work Experience:** Teaching (AAARGH!!!) at St Bartholomew's Primary. I tried reasoning with her that school is somewhere you want to get away from, not go back to for the rest of your life. But I think Abby will be an excellent teacher, just like my sister Daisy. (Oh dear, just mentioning Daisy's name makes me miss her. Marrying Diggory was inevitable, but moving to Scotland . . . When she was here I thought I'd give anything to see her go, but now she's not here – well, it is all a bit empty.)

**School:** Quite happy to be there for the rest of her life (groan!).

5

**Boyfriend(s):** James is still The One. Abby tells me he is doing his Work Experience at the White Hart Hotel in Borechester, clearing tables, peeling potatoes and washing up.

**Tracey:** MAD FRIEND!!! She is full of fun and makes the rest of us fall about. Sometimes she takes things too far and says things that make us FALL OUT. But she usually manages to bring us round by making us laugh again. Recently, however, she has become more serious . . .

TRACEY **Age:** 16

**Chosen Work Experience:** Working for a firm of solicitors called Hogsbreath, Whittle and Sneed. This is not quite as bad as being a teacher, but you have to wear SMART clothes (for SMART, read BORING), look

HOGSBREATH, WHITTLE AND SNEED

TRACEY IS WEARING A SUIT...

very serious and call a strange man in a wig 'Your Honour'. Tracey has started carrying a serious-looking briefcase around with her. We persuaded her to open it, and it was full of hair gel, hairspray, make-up, etc. Tracey tells me that you get paid loads for being a lawyer. I said that money isn't everything, and I would rather do something I love. That's why I am an artist. We nearly fell out again, so I decided to leave it.

**School:** Wants to return to school as she views it as an essential stepping-stone along her route to the loot (as a highly-paid, top lawyer).

**Boyfriend(s):** Back with Zak. Tracey tells us that Zak is doing his Work Experience at an estate agent's. She seems worried that he may have an office romance and go off with a glamorous estate agent – I tell her not to worry.

**Rowena:** Scary Friend – she is very sporty and STRONG, as I found out to my cost when I unwisely challenged her to an arm-wrestling contest. (My arm hung by my side like a limp rag for several hours afterwards, although she did say she was sorry and didn't mean to hurt me. I tend not to argue with her.) Rowena has had her head shaved. She says this enables her to run and swim faster as it cuts down on wind and water resistance. I resisted the urge to make rude remarks about wind resistance as she is a black and blue belt in Tai Kwon Do.

ROWENA

**Age:** Nearly 17 (getting old – or nearing her peak performance, as she would put it!)

**Chosen Work Experience:** Working at the local leisure centre, surrounded by hunky lifeguards and fitness trainers. HA! Call that work??! There is definitely method in Rowena's madness.

**School:** Says she may not bother going back, if they'll take her on full-time at the leisure centre.

**Boyfriend(s):** She recently split with Ed after he got in a serious stress because she could run faster than him, throw things further, etc. The final straw was when she beat him at weightlifting.

**Clare:** Quiet Friend (it's always the quiet ones, as they say . . .)

**Age:** 16. Occasionally more like 12. Occasionally more like 21. Confusing.

**Chosen Work Experience:** Assisting at the local vet's surgery. Clare likes animals. (You only have to look at her boyfriends – ha ha! Sorry, Clare! Please don't hit me.) Clare's parents are fiercely protective so the boyfriends tend not to last long (they get scared off . . .). I told her

CLARE

I wouldn't want to stick my arm up a cow's backside, but she said she would only be dealing with small, cuddly, furry creatures . . . (but then she looked worried).

**School:** Wants to go back. Does not want to leave. Says it's safer at school. Safer than what? Clare doesn't seem able to answer this.

**Boyfriend(s):** The more the merrier! The most recent ones were Nigel and Keith.

**Fabulosa:** New Friend (newer than my old friends!)

**Age:** Nearly 17

**Chosen Work Experience:** Working for *Tarte* magazine, a glossy and expensive publication, full of photos of famous people. The Fashion editor at *Tarte* is Fabulosa's cousin, and Fabulosa's dad has pulled strings to get her the job at *Tarte*'s London office, to and from which she will be chauffeur-driven every day. Her dad spoils her rotten, but he sometimes upsets her by interfering in her life too much. I should hate her and I did (we all did) at first, but we

FABULOSA

found out that she is just like the rest of us (and, possibly, nicer than the rest of us!). She is a great friend.

**School:** Likes it now that we are all friends (although she isn't sure about Tracey or Rowena). She hopes that we will not lose touch with each other after we leave school, and thinks that we should all stay there for as long as possible.

**Boyfriend(s):** Often shows us photos of hunky Italian boys, but insists they are 'just friends'.

**Mark:** Boyfriend (I think. Sometimes.)

**Age:** 16

MARK ← SPOTS

I keep worrying that I like him more than he likes me. Then I worry that he likes me more than I like him. I still hope that one day we will get it right because I really DO like him. Only I have gone off him recently because he keeps whistling in an annoying manner, and seems a bit full of himself. I hope that this is just a phase, as Mum would put it (I have been going through one phase after another, ever since I was born – in fact, I feel totally phased).

**Chosen Work Experience:** Something to do with computers. Working for a company called Total I.T. Enterprises in Plumbury (or T.I.T., for short, as Tracey helpfully pointed out). It sounds OK, I suppose, if you like computers (Mark does, but I find them BORING, so I try to stop him going on AND ON about them). Mark needs a well-paid job in the future so that he can support me and the kids. HA HA!!!

**School:** School is useful – he gets to see me every day!
**Girlfriend:** ME!

## Family

(Useful – or annoying, as the case may be – to come home to at the end of a hard day's work. I know I'm lucky to have their love and support, as well as to have my washing done and access to a well-stocked fridge . . . if my brothers haven't got there first and cleaned it out, etc., etc.)

## Dad

**Name:** Hank
(Embarrassing.)
**Age:** 147 (He was 146, but he has aged recently.)

Dad is brilliant with computers, but is very puzzled indeed by life (and by my life, in particular).

MUM — QUITE ATTRACTIVE AND WELL-PRESERVED — BUT FREQUENTLY STRESSED

## Mum

**Name:** Petunia Rose (Cringe. Double cringe.)
**Age:** Getting younger (or so she tells me).

Mum is always there when I need her (and also when I don't). Tends to moan that the house is not tidy and that she has too much to do, running her own interior design business and looking after all of us and sorting out our silly arguments (by which she means yelling 'SHUT UP!!!' at the top of her voice). I *do* help – last week I scraped the mould off a cup which had been sitting in a corner of the kitchen for MONTHS . . . She and Dad should chill out more (and get out more, leaving the house to ME).

## Siblings

Far too many of them, so having the house to myself is DIFFICULT.

ALEX! IF YOU'RE DRAWING ME AGAIN, I'LL...

## Big Sissy (a.k.a., Daisy Henrietta)
**Age:** 20

Daisy has gone, and I miss her! I try not to get upset about this because I know that Daisy is happy, and living in wedded bliss with Diggory the librarian – and I am glad. But how can she really, truly, be happy without ME!!!?! Doesn't she miss having me around, having me to talk to – OK, I mean having me to listen to? Doesn't she miss my funny little ways (borrowing her CDs, make-up, clothes, etc?). How is life possible without MEEEEE??!

## Recurring Nightmares
## (otherwise known as BROTHERS)

## Daniel Nathaniel Fitt

**Age:** 14

**Main characteristic:** Spotty, but occasionally shows signs of becoming human. I have felt closer to Daniel since Daisy left (but not too close, especially when he takes his trainers off – he should issue a government health warning. Extra pollutants in the stratosphere go up one hundred per cent! Some of my friends fancy him (they obviously haven't encountered his socks). This is worrying!

## Sebastian Jervase Fitt

**Age:** 12

**Main characteristic:** Snotty. No apparent signs of becoming human. Main objective in life is to be as annoying as possible.

## Henry Algernon Fitt

**Age:** 9

**Main characteristic:** Annoying. Hero-worships both his older brothers and wants to be just like them (i.e., annoying). Also likes Mark a lot and tends to hang around when Mark comes to the house to see me (MEGA-ANNOYING!!!).

## Smallest Sibling of Them All
## Rosie Clementine

**Age:** 5

My friends all think that Rosie is CUTE (these are the same poor deluded friends who think I am lucky to have so many brothers and sisters). She *is* pretty, with a mop of brown curls and big blue eyes. I love Rosie really, and I hope she thinks I'm the coolest big sister around. I've noticed she's started coming to me with her problems (OK, so the biggest problem so far was not being able to get the wrapper off a sticky lollipop). Rosie now goes to St Bart's Primary, and is VERY excited that Abby is going to be a classroom assistant there!

BABY
(AW... CUTE!)
(SOMETIMES)

## On with the diary . . .

**Alex's most recent School Experience:**

**Break-time**

I am on my knees, groping around in my school bag as I am in desperate need of an Eating Experience. Eventually I find a crushed packet of crisps and a squashed chocolate bar lurking under a maths textbook.

'Hi, Alex!'

'Oh, hello, Abby – I'm starving! You talk while I eat.'

'Alex! You're not *really* going to eat *that*?!'

'Mmmm . . . mmmm . . . mmmmm . . .'

'It'll be a relief to get out of here,' says Abby. Then, catching my eye: 'Not that I won't miss you, of course, Alex – but we'll catch up after work, won't we?'

'Yes, sure.' (I just hope Abby won't rave on about how

MMMM...
MMMM...
MMMM...

**EATING EXPERIENCE**

great it is being a teacher! Never mind – wait till she hears about life in a real, working ART STUDIO, which is where I'm going! I hope she won't be *too* jealous. I am going to be TOTALLY creative! It's an opportunity to give expression to the REAL ME.)

'I can't wait to start teaching those kiddies – they're so cute!' Abby continues. 'And I'll see your little sister there every day.'

'Lucky you. I can't wait to get away from my family, including Rosie. Especially Rosie. Yesterday she mixed loads of my make-up together in a toy saucepan and made "pie" for her toy rabbit.'

'Bless!'

'ABBY!!! That make-up cost loads! Rosie's a pain in the . . . ! You don't know how lucky you are, being an only child. Brothers and sisters can really get you down.'

'Alex – even my experience of being with *your* family hasn't put me off.'

(I am not sure how to take this, but I let it pass.) Abby and I are walking past Miss Tweedie's office. Miss Tweedie is the co-ordinator for our Work Experience. This sparks Abby into her obsessive checklist mode.

'I've just been through my Work Experience Checklist with Miss Tweedie,' Abby says.

'Oh,' I say, rather heavily, but Abby doesn't notice and carries on.

**MISS TWEEDIE**

16

'Miss Tweedie said she thought I'd be very good working with little children. And I promised I'd be punctual and not wear jeans, trainers or masses of jewellery. And that I'll take a packed lunch, and report to Mr Scribbling, the headmaster, when I arrive on my first day.'

'It'll be just like this place all over again, only smaller.' I say. 'I thought the whole point of Work Experience was to get away from school and all the rules. Sometimes I worry about you, Abby . . . So Miss Tweedie liked your choice?'

'Yes.'

'She didn't like *my* choice. I didn't even want to go and see her, but Mr Chubb made me. You should have seen her face when I said I wanted to be an artist. I might just as well have said I wanted to be a mad axe murderer. She asked me if I realised what a very uncertain area it was, and told me that I ought to consider getting another job as well, to supplement my income as an artist.'

'What did you say?'

'I said, "No thank you", and that I wished to commit myself to my art, twenty-four seven.'

'You said that?'

'Yes. Then she gave me this really strange look and turned to her computer, which had a fit and printed out eight pages on accountancy before she could stop it – she kept hitting it, and eventually she had to unplug it at the wall.'

'What happened next?'

'She told me to come back another time.'

Abby looks thoughtful. 'Still,' she says reflectively, 'Miss

Tweedie has a point – being an artist *is* an uncertain profession.'

'You sound like her. I may have one or two lean years, when I'm reduced to being a pavement artist. But then a wealthy American art collector will come along and like my work so much that he'll buy up the whole pavement and have it shipped out to the States in its entirety. After that, people will pay a fortune for my work, and I'll fly you, Tracey, Rowena and Clare out to my luxury home in the Bahamas at my expense.'

'Wow! What about Fabulosa?'

'She can afford to fly herself out there, whereas you'll just be a struggling schoolteacher.'

'Thanks, Alex.'

## Wednesday June 26th

**Break-time, again**

'Oh no – it's the Demon Whistler!'

'What?' Tracey asks. 'Oh – you mean Mark!'

Mark has taken to whistling endlessly and tunelessly – it is EXTREMELY irritating, and it is certainly making me re-think our relationship. I CANNOT go out with a compulsive whistler. But the moment he stops whistling I fancy him again!

'Mark seems really happy!' Rowena remarks.

'Too happy. Can't anyone say something depressing to him to stop him whistling?' I plead.

'Tell him it's over between him and you,' Tracey

suggests. 'That'll stop him whistling.'

'Yes – but if he stops whistling, I'll want to go out with him again.'

'And then he'll be happy and start whistling again . . .'

THE DEMON
WHISTLER

'Exactly.'

'Hmmm . . . it's a tricky one,' Tracey concedes.

Mark comes over and throws his arm around my shoulders.

'Hello, girls!'

'Hello, Mark. You seem happy.'

'I'm OK! I'm really looking forward to working for Total I.T. Enterprises in Plumbury next week.'

'T.I.T., for short,' Tracey points out again. 'Or T.I.T.E.'

'Whatever,' says Mark, the smile only fading from his face for a fraction of a second (it will take more than one rude remark from Tracey to depress him). 'It's one of the top computer companies in the country. They might even keep me on if I do really well. I might not bother coming back to school. Miss Tweedie said I've got a natural flair for working with computers – I fixed her computer for her.'

'So she liked you,' I remark, with only a hint of jealousy.

'I think so. She was the one who suggested Total I.T. I'm off to the I.T. room now – Mr Gribble's got problems with

the school's computer system, and he's asked *me* to help
him sort it . . .'

Mark wanders off, whistling.

'Your face says it all, Alex.' Tracey comments. 'Aren't
you pleased for Mark? He's supposed to be your boyfriend.'

'He is my boyfriend. I think. I hope. No! I mean – I'm not
sure what I mean.'

'He seems a lot happier and more confident now he's
found out what he wants to do with his life,' says Abby.
'That's good, isn't it?'

'Yes, I know,' I reply. 'Of course I'm pleased for Mark.
It's just . . . I'd be more pleased if he wasn't so pleased with
himself. And if it seemed to matter a bit more to him what
I thought. He hasn't even asked. I'd love to tell him I'm
pleased for him, if he gave me the chance. And if he'd just
stop whistling . . .'

## Thursday June 27th

**Home Experience**

Abby comes home with me after school. Rosie, my little
sister, rushes up to her and gives her a big hug.

'I can't wait till you come to my school, Abby!' she
exclaims. 'I've told all my friends you're coming, and they
can't wait either. Jonathan drew you a picture.' She hands
Abby a scrumpled piece of paper.

'Oh, that's really sweet!' says Abby, smoothing out the
drawing. 'Er . . . what is it?'

IT'S YOU BEING AN ALIEN!

'It's you!'

'Oh, wow! I'm . . . green!'

'It's you being an alien. And because green is Jonathan's favourite colour.'

'Right. Oh, Alex – they're so cute at that age, aren't they?'

I decide not to mention that yesterday Henry put a slug in my underwear drawer, and this morning Rosie drew rabbit ears and teeth in thick black felt tip marker on my FAVOURITE poster of super-sexy Brett Trousler, who doesn't look so good as a rabbit.

'Yes . . . Just wait till the kids get you covered in glue and paint and stuff.'

'I'll wear an apron.'

'An APRON?!'

'Yes, a painting apron, or overalls, or something.'

'Full protective clothing, I would think.'

'You'll need to wear an apron too, Alex. At the studio. Because of all the paint and stuff.'

'ABBY – artists do NOT wear aprons!!! They wear clothes that express their feelings and their mood. Wearing an apron would say to the world: "I am a very sad person who wears an apron . . ."'

'OK! OK!!! Forget I ever said anything about aprons!'

We sit in silence for a few moments. I hope I have not offended Abby. I can imagine her being the sort of schoolteacher whom all the children love, and it won't matter if she wears an apron, or not. I tell her this, and she smiles.

'I'm meeting Kaz this weekend,' I tell her.

'Kaz?'

'Kaz Wetherby-Trendle – she's really successful, and her paintings sell for loads of money. Mr Chubb said I should try to find out how she managed before she became successful. I'll probably find out more on Sunday. She's invited me over to her house for lunch, to see the studio and meet her family before I start work on Monday.'

'Cool!'

'Yes. I can't wait. I hope she likes me. I'm nervous – I've never met a live artist before!'

'What about a dead one?'

I give Abby a friendly push. 'Dad's giving me a lift,' I continue. 'It will be nice for him to see me commute like a real professional. Poor Dad! He never gets out – he just works from home.'

The phone rings in the hall. Mum rushes out of the kitchen to answer it.

'Daisy! How lovely to hear from you, darling! It's Daisy, Alex!'

'Yes – I sort of guessed.'

'Are you and Diggory settling into the house? Good . . .

good . . . and Diggory's new job? . . . good . . . good . . . Hang on, darling – something's burning in the kitchen! Talk to Alex, will you? I'll be back!' Mum thrusts a floury, slightly buttery receiver at me. 'Alex, talk to Daisy!'

I don't need asking twice – it seems like ages since I last spoke to Daisy.

'Hi, Daisy! I gather everything's good where you are. That's good. Me? Not bad, I suppose. I'm missing you . . . Hang on, Abby's doing a fish impression – she's mouthing something at me . . . Oh, she wants to know if you can give her some tips about teaching, because she's about to do her Work Experience at St Bart's. Here you are, Abby.

'Hello, Daisy, Oh . . . right! Yes . . . yes . . . yes. Thanks! Bye!'

Mum has returned to take over the phone. But I want to speak to Daisy again – I NEED to speak to her! I want to tell her that I'm missing her, and I need advice about Mark, and I'm sorry if I was ever a pain when she was living at

TALK TO ALEX . . . ALEX – TALK TO DAISY!

home . . . But Mum waves me away, flicking flour and bits of pastry at me. Life is so UNFAIR!

'What did Daisy say to you, Abby?' I ask as we retreat to my room. (I try not to sound reproachful, even though Abby used up what would have been my time on the phone to Daisy.)

'Daisy told me there was only one thing I need to remember: that if I can cope with *you*, Alex, I can cope with anything . . . Eeek!'

Very funny.

Abby and I agree to ask Tracey, Rowena and Clare to Abby's house on Saturday, so that we can talk about Work Experience and Other Things . . .

'Will it be all right with your mum if we all turn up?'

'Oh, yes – she likes it when I have friends round! She says it brings a bit of life into the house.'

## Friday June 28th

**Last day at school for two weeks!**

Abby and I are so excited that we skip down one of the corridors, hand in hand, not caring how stupid we look. Mr Chubb emerges from a nearby classroom.

'Ah – Alex and Abby! I'm glad to see that you're approaching your Work Experience fortnight with a cheerful and positive attitude! It seems like only yesterday that you were new to the school . . . I remember how nervous you were when you had to ask me the way to the Science Block . . .' Mr Chubb pulls a large white handkerchief out of his pocket. This is worrying – surely Mr Chubb is not going to start crying . . . !

SURELY MR CHUBB IS NOT GOING TO START CRYING . . . ?!

'Er, I think we're late for the next lesson, Sir – we've got to go!' We hurry away before Mr Chubb has a chance to get too emotional, and leave him blowing his nose loudly . . .

'Look out!' Turning the corner, we collide with Mark, who, for once, is not whistling. He is not even looking cheerful.

'What's the matter, Mark?' Abby asks.

I am aware of a shift in my feelings towards Mark – this is not unusual these days! He looks lost and vulnerable. Even if he's been a bit full of himself recently, I don't like to see him looking miserable. I want to put my arms around him. Uh-oh! Steady on!!!

'Bad news,' replies Mark, shaking his head. 'T.I.T. has gone *bust*.'

'You mean the bottom's dropped out of the market?' Abby asks, unexpectedly.

'Excuse me!' I exclaim. 'Am I missing something here? Why are you two jabbering on about busts and bottoms?'

'It's no joke, Alex,' Mark says sadly. Total I.T. Enterprises doesn't exist any more. The company's collapsed. It's gone bankrupt, right down the drain. My whole life's crashed.'

'HA!' I exclaim, loudly. (I immediately wish I was dead. I didn't mean to say 'HA!' like that. Sometimes things escape from my mouth before my brain has time to kick in.)

Abby stares at me, aghast. Mark looks astonished and hurt.

'No! No – I didn't mean . . .' I stammer. 'What I meant was, well, everyone's always telling me how uncertain it is being an artist, and what an unreliable job it is, and everything. But now it looks like being in computers is just as uncertain, doesn't it? On the other hand,' I add, looking at the unchanged expressions on Abby and Mark's faces, 'you could just ignore me. *Please* ignore me! I'm mad, OK? I'm an artist, you see. Take no notice.'

'Actually, I wanted to ask you something, Alex,' Mark says, mumbling slightly. 'Something important.'

(Is he going to ask me out? Or ask me to marry him?! It seems a strange moment to choose, especially now that his future is so uncertain.)

'Ask away!' I say brightly.

'Well . . .' Mark begins, hesitating. 'Because of what's happened – what I just told you about, only I'm not going to say it again in case you go "HA!" again . . .'

'Get on with it, Mark.'

'OK. I really need somewhere – urgently – to do my Work Experience. And now I know I want to work with computers, I was wondering if your dad could help. I know he has his own computer business . . .'

'Yes, sure. I expect he could make a few enquiries for you, ask around . . .'

'No – I don't think you quite get it, Alex. I want to work *with* your dad, helping him to run his business.'

'Er, you do? That would be quite . . . weird. But Dad's office is too small. You know he works in a room in our house?'

'Of course I *know*, Alex. I've been to your house, remember?'

'Yes – sorry! And I really like it when you come to my house. I mean . . .' (I feel myself going red in the face. AAARGH! The situation is getting seriously UNCOOL.) 'But . . . but the room's so small, and Mum has to get in there with the Hoover too!' I stammer.

'I wouldn't get in the way, Alex. And I'd offer to do the Hoovering for your mum. What's the matter? Don't you want me there?'

'No, no – of course I don't!'

'You don't?'

'NO – no, I mean, I don't mind. It's just . . . a surprise, that's all! I have to adjust . . .'

'Well, while you're adjusting, I'm off to have another word with Miss Tweedie and Mr Chubb. They say it's fine with them, as long as your dad says yes, and everything conforms to Health and Safety Regulations, which I'm sure it does.'

'Hmm . . . I'm not so sure about that. The cat's always being sick all over the place, and my brothers are totally unhygienic – especially Daniel's socks. And you should *see* the place before Mum's Hoovered. There's nothing safe or healthy about it. And then there's Rosie's Yellow Bunny . . . But if you're brave or mad enough . . .'

'Do you think I could come over later and talk to your dad? There isn't enough time left to write a letter. Will he be around later?'

'He usually is. I keep trying to persuade him and Mum to get out more . . .'

'I'll see you later, then!' Mark rushes off, looking more cheerful than he did, but not whistling (yet).

I am not sure how I feel. I am glad Mark is feeling happier, and I *like* him, but I don't think I am ready for him to Move In! There is also the Embarrassment Factor to consider. What will Mum and Dad say to Mark when I am not around to keep them under control?! Nightmarish visions of Dad giving Mark a lecture on duty, responsibility and proper behaviour towards his daughter float across my stressed brain, not to mention the unsettling thought of Mum bringing out albums with baby photos of me, etc., etc.

**Back home (and not a moment to lose . . .)**
I corner Dad in his office.

'Dad! Dad! It's about Mark! Dad! About Mark . . . !' I am out of breath and incoherent.

'Alex, calm down! Take a few deep breaths,' Dad advises. 'I know it's exciting.'

'What is?'

'Having your boyfriend here to do his Work Experience!' says Dad, digging me annoyingly in the ribs and giving me what he obviously thinks is a roguish wink. 'I bet you had something to do with this, didn't you, Alex? Eh? Eh?'

(This is BAD.)

'Dad! What's going on? How did you know . . . ?'

'I had a phone call from your school, a couple of hours ago. A nice lady called Miss Tweedie rang and explained the situation. She asked if I could help by taking him on for two weeks. I said "of course!"'

'You didn't.'

'I did! What's the matter? Aren't you pleased?'

'I'm not sure, Dad. I'll let you know . . .'

'Then I filled in some forms, made a few phone calls, and everything's set for Mark to join me next week. I rather like the idea of having a willing student working alongside me – it'll make a pleasant change from working on my own. And . . .' Dad taps the side of his nose and gives me another roguish wink. 'I knew how pleased you'd be if I said yes! I think you're just pretending to be upset. I know how you girls are!'

(NO, Dad, I don't think you do! And let's not get sexist, puh-*leeease*!)

'Oh dear!' I say quietly, leaning against a nearby wall.

Dad chuckles knowingly. (This is mega-annoying, since he knows *nothing*.)

'Mark's a friend, that's all,' I say. 'And he whistles. The whistling will drive you mad.'

Dad laughs. 'I'm sure we'll get on fine. I've always liked Mark. Nice boy. I get on well with his parents. And I think Mark can be trusted to behave well towards you.' (Here we go . . . ) 'Anyway, Alex, you won't be here much, will you? You'll be doing your own Work Experience.'

A "ROGUISH" WINK

THIS IS **BAD** . . .

This is a cheering thought. I won't be here. By the time I get home each evening, Mark should have gone, and I won't have to put up with Dad winking roguishly at us, or put up with Mum calling out things like, 'Alex, your boyfriend's here!'

**Later**

'Alex! Your boyfriend's here!'

'Mum! I expect Mark's here to see Dad about Work Experience.'

YOUR BOYFRIEND'S HERE!

Mark looks tidy, well scrubbed and slightly nervous.

'Since when have you been nervous of my dad?' I ask, trying to sound cool. (The effect is spoiled by the fact that I was halfway through spiking my hair, and it is sticking out at weird angles and flopping over my face, but I have to find out what's going on.)

'He's not just your dad any longer, Alex. He's my employer – with any luck.'

He knocks on Dad's office door, and I hear Dad's voice call out: 'Come in, Mark! . . . Not you, Alex.' The door is shut firmly in my face. This is getting silly . . .

**Half an hour later**
I hear footsteps on the stairs, and a familiar whistling.

'You got the job, then?' I say, emerging from my room.

'Yes!' Mark exclaims. 'Your dad's the best, Alex! He's just rebooted my entire life.'

'That's . . . great. I'm pleased. Really I am . . . it's great to see you looking so . . . rebooted.' (I can't help wishing that someone or something would reboot me. I don't feel at all happy about Mark working for Dad!)

31

## Saturday June 29th

**The last girlie get-together before Work Experience!**

It is a strange and scary thought that on Monday we will all be working women, no longer controlled by power-crazed teachers and the insistent clanging of the school bell! (OK, so the school bell rings rather than clangs, but I have been told by the school that I may record my thoughts and feelings about Work Experience in the form of poetry.) No more timetable! No more Mr Chubb! (Strangely, the last thought is a sad one.) Will any of us ever want to go back? How can I possibly adjust from being a free-spirited artist back to the school routine again? How do my friends feel about it all? After an hour or so of free-ranging discussion. I came to the conclusion that we are all either: excited, worried, happy, nervous, or all of the afore-mentioned.

Clare looks especially uneasy. She says she is concerned that she has made the wrong choice in opting to work at the vet's. Abby says that this is probably P.W.E.S. (Pre-

DEEFER DOG

Work Experience Syndrome). Rowena doesn't help by telling Clare that her cousin Rodney is going to bring Deefer, his old English Sheepdog crossed with a Spaniel to the vet. Deefer is the hairiest dog in existence, and he likes to eat vets.

The evening is a laugh until Abby goes all serious and teacher-like and tells us to help tidy her room. So we have to beat her up with cushions and pillows. Tracey's bun explodes, so that her hair is sticking out at all angles. Clare gets slightly hurt when several of my spikes dig into her (they are *very* stiff . . .).

**TRACEY'S BUN EXPLODES**

'It's going to be so cool, not going to school for a whole fortnight!' I exclaim when it is time for us to leave.

## Sunday June 30th

At last! Today's the day when things really start to happen! I am both nervous and excited at the thought of meeting a real, living artist, who will also be my employer for the next two gloriously school-free weeks!

**TODAY'S THE DAY ...**

**Thought:** Will she like my hair?

**Next thought:** Don't be stupid! Forget the hair! Will she like the rest of me?

**Another thought:** Will she like my work? I'm taking my art folder, with all my best drawings in it.

**Unworthy thought:** I don't want to do this any more. I'll say I'm sick. I want to work in a supermarket, stacking shelves . . .

**Angry thought:** What is my *problem*??! I am an ARTIST. I can do anything! It doesn't even matter if she likes my work, or not . . .

I am saved from further thoughts by the ringing of my mobile. It is Abby, who sounds as though she is panicking even more than I am.

'What if the children don't like me, Alex?'

'They'll love you, Abby – don't worry about it.'

'But you've got loads more experience than I have in dealing with children. You've got all those brothers and sisters.'

'Don't I know it. Hang on – there's one of them listening

34

outside my door. I HATE it when they do that . . . DANIEL?! Is that you? It had better not be, or I'll squish you flat! I'm still bigger than you, remember? So take a running jump! And take Seb with you – I can hear him making those noises he makes, like a chimp that's swallowed helium. And take Henry with you too. AND Rosie – yes, Rosie, Yellow Bunny has to go too. Tell Yellow Bunny it's not NICE to listen through doors!'

I march over to the door and open it, which is enough to send them all screaming down the stairs like a herd of small elephants. (Am I THAT frightening?) Then I remember that Daniel is growing fast and will soon be bigger than me – I had better be nice to him!

'Sorry, Abby – I think they've gone now . . .'

'Hmm . . .' says Abby, as we resume our conversation. 'I'm not sure that approach would go down well at St Bart's. Frightening little children and squishing people flat is frowned on, so I'm told.'

'Abby, you'll be fine! You're a natural with children, much better than I am! Rosie thinks you're wonderful. So just be yourself. But I've really got to go now. Dad and I are leaving in about half an hour to go to Kaz's place . . . I'm having lunch there, remember? I'll get to see the studio, and meet her family . . . Yes – I'm nervous! . . . OK, I'll just be myself. At the moment I'm being myself with bad hair. I've only spiked half my head so far, and it looks stupid. I'll call you when I get back, OK? Try and relax! Bye, Abby!'

**Half an hour later. It is time to go . . .**

'Have you been to the loo yet, Alex?'

'MUM!!! I'm not a little kid!'

'No – I mean, have you been in the downstairs loo to look at the painting behind the door? It's one of Kaz's. She gave it to me nearly ten years ago. But don't tell her I hung it in the loo.'

'You mean that green and gold painting? I didn't know it was one of hers.'

'Yes, it is.'

'It looks a bit like a lizard. Or a dragon. It's something green, anyway. But I'd better go now – I don't want to be late! Bye, Mum!'

'Good luck, darling! Give Kaz my love. She's really nice – you'll like her.'

The journey by car to Plumbury is straightforward until we get caught up in Plumbury's complicated one-way system, which carries us straight past the intersection we need. I takes several tries before Dad, who is getting mildly stressed, manages to find a way of approaching the same road from a different direction.

'Tomorrow I think I'll let the train take the strain,' I comment.

'You saw the sign to the station?' Dad asks. 'Looks like it's not *too* far from the town centre – about a ten-minute walk, I'd say. Ah, here we are.'

Kaz's house is a tall and imposing town house, with

36

green railings and a flight of stone steps leading up to a bottle-green front door.

'She really likes green! Dad, thanks for bringing me today, but you don't need to hold my hand!'

'I'm just guiding you up the steps, Alex. I'll say hello to Kaz and find out when I should come back. Then I'll say goodbye and disappear.'

A tall lady with long, curly, fair hair, wearing a green and gold-trimmed Indian style tunic over baggy purple trousers, gathered at the ankle, and bare feet, opens the door.

'Hank! How good to see you again after all this time! Won't you come in? And this must be Alex! Goodness me! The last time I saw you, I think you must have been about five years old. You had a mop of golden curls
– and now you have spikes!'

'Er, yes!'

'I won't stay, Kaz,' says Dad. 'I think Alex would prefer it if I didn't hang around. I'm just the chauffeur today!'

I stand there, grinning foolishly, until Dad has gone. (I realise too late that I have left my art folder behind in the car. Never mind – I will bring it next week.)

'Come and meet my family, Alex!'

YOU HAD A MOP OF GOLDEN CURLS!

says Kaz, leading me by the hand into a green and gold drawing room, with tall French windows opening out on to a stone terrace that overlooks a long, narrow garden full of strange sculptures, including an enormous bronze sail. In the shade cast by this sail is tethered a large, hairy brown beast, grazing quietly among the flower beds. (I find myself wishing that Mark was here – he'd love all this! But what IS that weird animal?)

'That's Gloria, our pet yak,' says Kaz, matter-of-factly. (Did she read my thoughts?) 'She gets a bit hot and cross in this weather, so it's probably best not to pet her.' (Like I was going to...)

'This is my husband, J,' Kaz says, introducing me to a man whose long

GLORIA

greying hair is tied back in a ponytail.

'J' raises his hand in greeting.
'Peace, sister!' he says.
(Somehow I cannot bring myself
to say, 'Peace, J!' Neither does
'It's nice to meet you, Mr
Wetherby-Trendle!' seem at
all appropriate, under
the circumstances. So I say nothing, and I am aware of the
foolish grin returning to my face . . .)

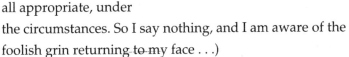

J WETHERBY-TRENDLE

'Meet my children, Alex. They're twins – about two years older than you. This is Orion and this is Aurelia.'

'Hi, Alex!' Aurelia is pretty, with long, fair hair like her mother, and she seems friendly. Orion, on the other hand, bears a passing resemblance to Gloria the yak. I cannot see his eyes under a heavy fringe of dark brown hair, hanging over his face like a curtain. He makes a sort of grunting noise, like a yak's. I think it is his way of saying hello.

ORION

AURELIA

'This is Alex, everyone!' says Kaz, putting her arm around me. 'She's come to do her Work Experience in the studio. You must call me Kaz, Alex. Everyone else does. We're all very relaxed here – there's good karma. Alex, I can feel your aura!'

'Wh . . . wh . . . where?!?' I jump in alarm, looking around me nervously.

Kaz laughs. 'Relax, Alex! It's nothing to worry about. Stand still. There's a good girl . . .' Kaz places her hands close to my head and moves them around, as if touching an invisible halo surrounding me.

'It's such a strong aura that I can see it – the colours are bright . . .'

'Kaz has a special gift which enables her to see auras,' J explains.

'Yes, you've certainly got the soul of an artist,' Kaz continess. 'Sensitive, passionate . . .'

'Er, thanks!' (The foolish grin is out of control – I am afraid I must look totally manic.)

'I remember my Work Experience,' Aurelia remarks. 'Herding yaks in Northern Tibet.'

(Well, that certainly makes washing brushes at the studio or sweeping up dogs' toenail clippings at the local vet's look rather tame.)

'Let's go and eat,' says Kaz. 'Then I'll show you the studio, Alex.'

'Great!'

J leads the way into a sort of conservatory built on to the side of the house. There is no table, but a big colourful rug is spread on the floor, covered with dishes piled high with different foods, not all of which I recognise.

'It's completely vegetarian, of course,' says Kaz. 'But not

one hundred per cent vegan. I hope that's OK with you, Alex.'

'It's fine, really!'

'And strictly no alcohol. I'm afraid I cannot allow you any fermented yak's milk.' (Thank God for that!)

'Will you say grace, J?'

'Certainly, my desert flower.'

The whole family sit cross-legged on the floor and bow their heads. I do the same. (Perhaps it is just as well Mark is not here – we would probably start laughing and make fools of ourselves!)

'For what we are about to receive, may the Lord (or whichever deity we may or may not subscribe to) make us fully globally aware,' J intones.

'Amen!'

'Alex, try a stuffed toadsquash! Don't be put off by the name – they're delicious!'

'Er, thanks – I think I'll have a banana.'

Orion lies on his front, propping himself up on his elbows as he chews at something disgusting and green.

'Orion! Elbows off the rug! How many times do I have to tell you! And we have a guest!' barks Kaz, turning abruptly and without warning from Kaz the Artist into Mrs Wetherby-Trendle the Mother.

I realise that I am utterly confused. I don't know whether I should act casual and laid-back, or whether I should sit up and mind my manners. Judging by the expression on Kaz's face as she glares at her son, I decide to mind my manners. Kaz may be a famous artist – but she is also a parent . . .

After lunch, J goes to meditate on the terrace and Aurelia carries a sloshing bucket of water down the steps for Gloria the yak. Orion has disappeared somewhere.

'Come and see the studio, Alex!' Kaz calls to me, climbing a circular open staircase leading from the terrace to the top of the building. 'This is a fire escape, by the way. It's important that you know that, because of Health and Safety Regulations. Don't worry – I'm not expecting a fire!'

Slightly out of breath, I reach the top of the staircase and step into a huge room, which covers the whole of the top floor – several rooms must have been made into one. It has an arched glass roof, so that you can see the sky.

'I must have natural light,' Kaz explains. 'But there are blinds, in case it gets too hot. And one or two of the glass panels in the ceiling can be opened, to let in air, as well as the windows over there. Have a look around, Alex.'

There are stacks of paintings everywhere – mostly of weird and wonderful creatures and mysterious shapes, curling and twisting and merging. One particularly large canvas rests on an easel, and there are pots of paint all over the place, most of them different shades of green. There are cupboards, sinks and draining boards down the entire length of one wall. In one corner, there is a desk, a computer and a photocopier.

'My agent, Robert, comes in once or twice a week. So you'll meet him. We're preparing for an exhibition at Plumbury Fine Arts at the moment, so you'll be involved in that too. You'll be at the gallery for some of the time. It won't just be washing brushes and sweeping!'

Kaz shows me where everything is – brushes, brush cleaner, jars, palettes, cloths, dustpan and brush, brooms, floor mops, phone, kettle, herbal tea bags and, more importantly, the biscuit tin. Unfortunately, the only biscuits in the tin are called Mucksters Sugar-free Bran Bars, which look like narrow strips of corrugated cardboard (and corrugated cardboard would probably taste better than these biscuits). The fridge is even less encouraging, containing only yak's yogurt (LOTS of yak's yogurt). (I must remember to bring a packed lunch.)

I am instructed how to answer the phone, and told to re-direct calls to the gallery if Kaz is busy painting UNLESS the calls are from Robert, Nigel or the Big Chief Clapper. I decide that it is better not to ask who or what the Big Chief Clapper is at this stage, as Kaz has started painting, and I have already been asked not to interrupt when she is working.

'And there may be a call from the vet's, Alex dear,' Kaz

says, over her shoulder. (She is allowed to talk while she is working – I am not.) 'About Gloria's booster jabs. And the hoof-trimming and de-ticking. Switch on the CD player, would you, please? Let's listen to "Peaceful Nature Sounds" while we work . . . could you rinse out all those jars over there . . . ?'

By the time Dad arrives to collect me, I am almost asleep, my senses lulled by the sound of wind in the trees and birds twittering ('Peaceful Nature Sounds'), and my mind numbed by the sheer monotony of rinsing out jar after jar after jar . . .

Kaz is so absorbed in her painting that she hardly seems to notice when I leave, and says, 'Goodbye, dear!' in a faraway, dreamy sort of voice.

'So, how was it?' Dad asks, as we drive home.

'Interesting,' I reply. 'They have a pet yak. Can we have a pet yak, Dad?'

'No. We haven't got room for a yak. Fancy them having a yak! But I don't want any animals – we've already got your brothers. So what else happened?'

'Not much. Do you mind if I just close my eyes for a while? I feel tired . . .'

Back home, I call Abby.

'Well?' says Abby. 'How did it go?'

'They're all completely mad!' I reply. 'Daft as brushes – ha ha! But friendly. They've even got a pet yak called Gloria!'

'A yak?!'

'Yes! And it goes to the vet. I must phone Clare and tell her. It's about time we had a good yak on the phone! HA HA!'

'Alex, you sound a bit hyper. Are you OK?'

'Sorry – I'm just making up for being nearly asleep earlier.'

'Why? Were you bored?'

'Nooo . . . not exactly. I'm sure it will get more interesting. I mean, I haven't really started at the studio yet – that's tomorrow . . .' (Who am I trying to convince – myself or Abby?) 'Yes, I'm sure it's going to be really exciting! And it's definitely better than school. And I'll even be working at an art gallery!'

'It sounds like your sort of thing, Alex – I bet you get to meet all sorts of people!'

'Yes! That's right! And Kaz is going to introduce me to her agent. That's what I need – an agent. I must remember to take my work with me to show him. He might put me on his books, and then I'd never need to go back to school again.'

'Oh, Alex, I wish you wouldn't say that! It's bad enough that Rowena doesn't want to go back . . .'

'That's only if she gets offered a permanent job at the leisure centre.'

'Yes, I know. But even so . . . you're making me nervous, and I'm already stressed enough about tomorrow. I couldn't stand it if you left school, Alex! Having you there makes it seem . . . right. It wouldn't be right if you weren't there.'

'OK, Abby – don't stress! You'll be fine tomorrow, and I promise I won't rush into anything like leaving school. It wouldn't seem . . . right, would it?'

## Monday July 1st

**Day One of Work Experience!!!**
(This is now my unofficial Work Experience Diary – the full, unexpurgated version, not suitable for persons of a nervous disposition, such as Mr Chubb . . . I also have a Logbook from the school to fill in each day, recording what I do and how I feel about it.)

I LEAP OUT OF BED . . .

**6 a.m.** Both my alarm clocks go off (I am taking no chances), and I leap out of bed. I actually LEAP OUT OF BED! I must stress how very unusual this is. My normal reaction to an alarm clock ringing is to bang it blindly with my hand to stop it, knocking everything else off the shelf where I keep it, and then hide under the bedclothes.

But today the Getting Up Experience is very different. I am very excited and looking forward to my first day at work, even though I didn't sleep much last night (too excited – and nervous).

I *think* Kaz liked my hair, although she also mentioned the 'golden curls' I had when I was little. (I am *not* having golden curls, even for Kaz . . .) So I spend some time spiking my hair, but I am not sure if I can face doing this *every* morning.

Looking out of the window I can see that it is going to be another hot day, so I put on a short top and flared jeans which I have decorated all over with badges and patches – suitably artistic, I think, and definitely an improvement on the SMART and SENSIBLE clothes my friends have to wear!

**7 a.m.** The rest of the family is beginning to wake up. I dance around Daniel and Seb's room, singing, 'Wake up! Wake up! It's a beautiful day!'

GOOD MORNING, DAD! HI, MUM! YOU'RE BOTH LOOKING GOOD!

'Eurrgh! Shut up! Go away! Get lost, Alex!'

(What is their problem? Anyone would think it was a crime to be cheerful in the morning . . . although I vaguely remember losing my temper with Dad once because he was being insufferably cheerful in the morning – but that was in the dim and distant past before I changed from a sulky teenager into Super Working Woman, intent on getting to her exciting and challenging job, the first step on the high-speed escalator to success and stardom!!!)

'Hello, Alex.'

'Good morning, Dad! Hi, Mum! You're both looking good!'

Dad gives me a strange look, and retires to the bathroom. Mum gently strokes my spikes.

'Don't touch my hair ! No one touches my hair!'

'There's no need to be prickly, Alex,' says Mum. 'That was a joke, by the way!' Now it is Mum's turn to be insufferably cheerful. 'I hope you have a lovely day, darling – have you got your rail fare, and your railcard, and a timetable? Have you taken your vitamins? Have you had breakfast? What time do you need to leave? I can run you to the station . . .'

'Mum! Stop fussing! I've got everything I need, and I don't want a lift. There's plenty of time, and I'm going to power walk to the station.'

'Well, if you're sure . . .'

**7.40 a.m.** I am just about to power walk out through the front door, when Mark arrives, slightly out of breath.

'You're early!' I remark. 'Dad isn't even downstairs yet.'

'I didn't want to be late for work,' Mark explains. 'I was awake all night waiting for my alarm to go off!'

I POWER WALK TO THE STATION...

'You need to relax, Mark,' I say. 'If you drive yourself too hard, you'll have a heart attack. You're more at risk if you have a sedentary job, such as sitting on your bum in an office all day staring at a computer.'

'Thanks, Alex.'

'I've got to go. Kaz needs me in the studio. Help yourself to cornflakes, Mark! Oh – and good luck!'

'I can't eat my employer's cornflakes, Alex – that's not right!'

'Oh, don't be silly! Cornflakes are one of the perks of the job, along with the company car. See you later!'

'Good luck, Alex!' Mark calls after me.

On the way to the station (I am on Maximum Power Walk! Walking fast helps me to stop feeling nervous!) I send 'good luck' text messages to all my friends, even Fabulosa. My friends send 'good luck' messages back to me, and then my phone rings. It is Fabulosa.

'Darling! I am in the car, on my way to work. Bruno the

chauffeur is so sweet. He has squeezed me . . .' It is quite hard to hear what she is saying, as it is a bad signal and her words are all clipped.) '. . . some fresh orange juice . . .' The phone goes dead.

### At the station

I am quite out of breath by the time I reach the ticket booth and produce my Young Person's Railcard. Never mind that the photo in my railcard makes me look like a hardened criminal likely to re-offend at any moment. It feels strange standing in a queue with all the other commuters, mostly businessmen in suits. I feel slightly self-conscious about my hair.

YOUNG PERSON'S RAILCARD
NAME: ALEX FITT
D.O.B: 25 . 5 . 86
CARD No: 0006780
EXP. DATE: 30 . 5 . 03

← PHOTO TAKEN IN BOOTH WHEN I WAS NOT READY (BUT DID NOT WANT TO WASTE MONEY HAVING IT DONE AGAIN)

I crowd on to the platform with the other passengers, who glance at their watches occasionally and then stand motionless and expressionless, staring into the middle distance. There is an announcement:

'The next train due at Platform 2 will be for Borechester, Plumbury, Spurge, Fluxham and Gorbling Sands. This train is running approximately ten minutes late.'

'Only ten minutes!' I hear one man exclaim. 'That's not bad.'

HAD A NASTY FRIGHT, LOVE?
YOUR HAIR'S STANDING ON END!
HARR
HARR
HARR!!!

THE GUARD

## On the train

At last I am on the train. I am lucky to get a seat, the only one available – but shortly afterwards I give it up for an old lady with a shopping basket, as she looks frail and I am afraid she may fall over as the train lurches out of the station (we have very old rolling stock on our line).

'Thank you, dear!' she says, smiling at me.

A while later, the guard approaches. He is a big man with bushy orange sideburns and a gap-toothed grin (bordering on a leer). 'Tickets, please!' The guard stamps my ticket and looks at my hair. 'Had a nasty fright, love? You're hair's standing on end! HARR HARR HARR!!!'

I grin weakly.

'I think your hair looks very nice, dear!' says the old lady

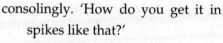

consolingly. 'How do you get it in spikes like that?'

'Hair gel, and spray.'

'Ah . . . my Rex used Brillocreem all his life, till his hair fell out. Rex swore by Brillocreem, he did. He didn't have spikes, though . . .' She carries on talking, partly to herself, partly to me, and I would probably drop off to sleep if I wasn't so nervous and excited about the day ahead. I am *sure* it will be more interesting than yesterday.

'Excuse me!' We have reached Borechester, and I am suddenly aware of a good-looking boy with short brown hair squeezing past me to get to the door. 'This is my stop.'

I notice that he is carrying a large art folder, and I watch out of the window as he walks away from the train. Suddenly he glances back over his shoulder right at me, and I look away quickly, embarrassed that he must have seen that I was watching him . . . (An image of Mark, looking hurt and reproachful, floats into my mind. For goodness sake! I was only LOOKING!!!)

I make a mental note to remind Mum to remind me to bring my art folder with me tomorrow (to show to Kaz and her agent . . . and *if* the good-looking boy were to be on the train again and *maybe* notice me with my art folder, that would be . . . nice . . . and it wouldn't hurt anyone . . .)

**At the studio**

My first day at Kaz's studio is uneventful. After we have

been through the Health and Safety Checklist (Kaz shows me the fire escape – again – and I ask where the loo is), she spends all her time painting (what is it they say about watching paint dry?) and listening to the CD of 'Peaceful Nature Sounds', which makes me want to go to sleep again, apart from the watery bits, which make me want to go to the loo (so it is just as well I asked where it was). (Why didn't I bring my walkman? Mum should have reminded me . . .) I do a lot of sweeping and making coffee (decaffeinated) and Heavenly Herbal tea, which smells disgusting. To my horror, there is fresh yak's milk yogurt for lunch.

'We have Gloria to thank for this!' enthuses Kaz.

*Why* didn't I remember to bring a packed lunch? Why didn't Mum make me one? (I was too busy spiking my hair and preparing myself mentally for the day ahead.)

There isn't a single visitor to the studio. No customers, no agents, no reporters, not even a wealthy American art collector. The phone rings only once, and I am sent to answer it. It turns out to be a wrong number.

In my Work Experience Logbook there is a section for me to fill in Key Skills, such as Communication (talking to other staff or members of the public, and using the telephone, for instance) and Working With Others. At this rate, I am going to have NO EXPERIENCE of either of these!

Another Key Skill is Information Technology, so I ask if

I can use the solitary computer in the corner of the studio. 'Can I write any letters for you, or print anything out?' I ask, hopefully.

'Oh, Robert does all that!' Kaz replies. 'He's the only one who can get that computer to work. Wait a few minutes, Alex, and I'll show you how to wash the brushes, but not my special brushes – only *I* wash those. And I only use organic turpentine.' (I can hardly contain my excitement.)

**Back on the train**

The same guard checks my ticket on the train journey home. 'Had a nasty fright, love? Your hair's standing on end! HARR HARR HARR!' (Is he going to crack the same 'joke' *every* day?) I look around for the good-looking boy, but he is nowhere to be seen.

**Back home**

I fend off Mum and Dad's volley of questions about how I got on by telling them that I feel tired and would they mind if I talked about it another time? I don't want to admit to anyone (apart from Abby, possibly) that I've had a really boring day. Artists aren't supposed to have boring days. It doesn't fit with my image – it doesn't go with the hair! I change the subject by asking about Mark. I feel sorry that I didn't get to see him, and that I was a bit abrupt this morning. (Hang on! – am I feeling guilty about something?)

'Mark was like a hyperactive flea in a fit this morning!'

Dad tells me. 'Mum and I kept trying to stop him, but we couldn't. Then, after lunch, he fell asleep face down on the photocopier, so I sent him home. The poor boy got quite upset – thought he'd been sacked. I managed to reassure him . . .'

I call Abby and ask how her day went.

'It was good,' she says. 'The children are lovely. One little boy wanted to sit on my lap all the time . . .'

'I know – that was Jonathan, wasn't it? Rosie told me. Rosie said you're the Best Teacher Ever!'

'That's really nice. But I am soooooo tired, Alex! I didn't sleep much last night. Do you mind if we catch up tomorrow? Are you OK? How's life as an artist?'

'Er . . . cool. It's fine.'

'Come round tomorrow, if you can, when you get back. Fabulosa's coming straight here from work, and so are Tracey, Rowena and Clare, if they're not too tired.'

## Tuesday July 2nd

**Day Two of Work Experience**

**6.30 a.m.** I have decided to allow myself an extra half-hour of sleep. Getting up at six was too extreme.

I go to the bathroom to do my hair. I am determined to keep the spikes as I am not going to let a stupid guard on a train embarrass or intimidate me!

Back in my room, I search through my bottom drawer and find a large, purple woolly hat, which covers my

spikes without crushing them. (This means it sits rather high on my head – I hope it doesn't look too strange, and the weather is almost unbearably hot . . .) I also remember my walkman AND my art folder. I even prepare myself a packed lunch, consisting of cheese and pickle sandwiches, a packet of crisps and three bars of chocolate. I feel ORGANISED. Everything is SORTED. It is a good feeling.

A LARGE, PURPLE WOOLLY HAT . . .

**7.45 a.m.** Mark arrives. 'I overslept!' he bleats, anxiously.

'Mark!' I say, putting a calming, well-organised hand on his shoulder. 'Dad isn't even awake yet. I think you wore him out yesterday. So don't stress! Dad's really pleased with you . . .'

'He is?' Mark's face brightens.

'Yes – really pleased. Er, I'm sorry about rushing off and not staying to talk. I wish you could see where I'm working. There's a yak called Gloria.'

'Really? That's . . . bizarre.'

'I've got to go, Mark. Let's catch up soon.'

'Yes, I'd like that. I miss not seeing you at school every day.'

'Yes, me too. Bye, Mark!' (Oh dear. Mark is being really NICE. That makes me feel WORSE about being attracted to the bloke on the train.)

'See you later, Alex! I won't fall asleep today, so I should still be here when you get back. I'm thinking of putting in some overtime, to make up for yesterday.'

'Oh . . . good.'

## On the train (which is running twenty minutes late)

'Tickets, please! . . . I like your tea cosy! HARR HARR HARR!!!'

Everyone in the packed carriage is staring at me as the guard grins proudly at his latest 'joke'.

I have had enough. 'Look!' I say to him fiercely. 'I don't make personal remarks about *you* . . .'

'OK! OK!' The guard holds up his hands in mock surrender. 'Keep your hair on! HARR HARR HARR!!!'

He wanders away, still laughing.

I turn up the volume on my walkman. Someone taps me on the shoulder. It is the guard (again). 'Put that away, love! This is a "Personal Stereo-Free Zone"! The other passengers don't appreciate the noise! You call it music, but I daresay there's a lot of us who wouldn't agree with that description! HARR HARR HARR!!!'

Grabbing my art folder and the bag containing my lunch, I decide to move to another carriage, away from the guard.

Collapsing into the only available seat in the next carriage, I find myself sitting opposite the good-looking boy with the art folder.

'Hello,' he says, smiling.

'Hello!' I reply, smiling.

We carry on smiling. My face begins to ache. I look out of the window, feigning sudden interest in the passing trees, sheep, etc. With a small pang of dismay, I remember that I am wearing a purple tea cosy on my head. No wonder he's smiling! I snatch it off my head and stuff it in my bag . . .

'Are you at the art college?' he asks suddenly. 'It's just – well, I don't think I've seen you . . .'

'No, I don't go to college.'

'Oh, right. But you've got a folder – sorry, I hope you don't think I'm being nosy . . .'

'Oh, no! Not at all. I'm just an artist.'

'Really? Cool! That's what I want to be, when I leave college. But it's hard to get started. So I'm doing bar work. You look very . . . young – sorry . . .'

'Um, it's OK. I often get told I look young for my age.' I clear my throat. 'There was this wealthy American art collector – he liked my work . . .' (What am I saying?! I say really weird things when I'm nervous!)

'Wow! Did he buy any of it?' he asks.

'Er, yes. One or two things.' (Can we change the subject, please? But my brain has gone hyper. I can't think of a single NORMAL thing to say. For some reason I want to say, 'I'm also an Arctic explorer and I recently wrestled a polar bear – and won.')

'Are you pulling my leg?' he asks.

'No! Well . . . only a little bit. But I'm working in a studio with another artist.'

'And that's for real?'

THERE WAS THIS
WEALTHY AMERICAN
ART COLLECTOR...

HARRY ( SWOON ! )

'Yes.' (Phew! I feel I've just had a narrow escape from total weirdness. Must calm down. Take deep breaths. Think of Mark . . .)

'Lucky you! Where?'

'Plumbury.'

'Nice one! I think I'm jealous! My name's Harry, by the way, and this is my stop. I'm at Borechester College of Art. And your name is . . . ?'

'Alex!'

'See you, Alex!'

'See you, Harry!'

Wow! I mean, that was nice. Harry's nice. He's REEEALLY nice! Oh no – stop it! We were just being friendly. Mark's my boyfriend, isn't he? Why am I asking myself that question?! I don't know the answer. I need Abby. And I need Daisy . . .

**At the studio**

'You look happy today, Alex!' Kaz comments. 'Your aura is golden. Are you in love?'

'Er . . .' I feel myself blushing furiously. 'What would you like me to do?' I ask, quickly, changing the subject.

'Could you rinse out these jars, please, Alex? This one's had Ox Gall Liquid in it – but don't worry, Alex, it's totally synthetic. Not a single ox was harmed in the manufacturing process.'

'That's good.'

'And while you're working, would you mind if I painted your aura?'

'Er . . . no. I mean, yes! That's fine.'

I feel I might as well not be there at all, as the day settles into the same snore-inducing routine as yesterday . . .

## ALEX'S EXCITING DAY AT THE STUDIO!

**9.30 a.m.** Scrub furiously at jar which contained Ox Gall Liquid. Am asked by Kaz to scrub more quietly and carefully. Am informed in a strained tone of voice by Kaz that I have accidentally flicked water on to the canvas she is working on.

**9.40 a.m.** Make mug of Heavenly Herbal tea and put on CD of 'Peaceful Nature Sounds' to soothe troubled artist.

**9.50 a.m.** Get Hoover out of cupboard. Am instructed to put Hoover away IMMEDIATELY, and use broom and dustpan and brush instead.

**10.30 a.m.** Utterly exhausted by over half an hour of intensive sweeping. Not a speck of dust left on the floor. Grab lunch box and eat sandwiches. Am informed by Kaz that I have made crumbs on the floor.

**10.40 a.m.** More sweeping.

**10.45 a.m.** Mop floor with Organic Hint of Heaven Pinefresh floor cleaner. Get into trouble for mopping too close to Kaz's feet – she points out that she could slip and fall over when she stands back to look at her canvas. She asks if I am bored. I assure her that I am not! (Then I wonder if I should have been more honest.)

**11.00 a.m.** Stand staring into middle distance. Am requested to go and DO SOMETHING.

**11.05 a.m.** Phone rings. It is the vet's surgery, wanting to know how old Gloria is. I ask Kaz. She holds up two fingers. I assume this means that Gloria is two years old and that Kaz is not being rude to me. I am beginning to feel depressed. Doesn't she like me?

**11.30 a.m.** Apparently the painting of my aura is going well, and Kaz is in a more buoyant mood. She celebrates by opening a bottle of Organic Essence of Elderflower and Cow-parsley Cordial, which I am invited to share with her. It looks (and smells) like the water in Dad's homemade water butt after Henry and Rosie have tipped buckets of mud and God knows what else into it. I quietly pour it down the plughole when Kaz has gone back to her painting.

**Rest of the Morning:** I am kept busy photocopying some publicity material about Kaz and her work, folding it, putting it into envelopes, stamping them and sticking on pre-printed address labels (which Robert has done on the computer and left in a pile for me). Unfortunately Kaz has never heard of self-sealing envelopes, and I am expected to lick well over a hundred Organic Recycled Better World Envelopes.

**1.00 p.m.** I feel sick (I have managed ninety-four envelopes and the world seems a much worse place as far as I am concerned). Unfortunately Kaz chooses this moment to shove a large pot of yak's yogurt under my nose with a cry of, 'Help yourself, Alex!' I rush to the loo and hide there for about half an hour. (I've heard of 'going green' – but not literally . . .)

**The afternoon:** The afternoon is largely a repeat of the morning, with the added thrill (sarcasm) of cleaning several dozen paintbrushes of assorted sizes. Kaz breathes down my neck while I do this, as she wants to make sure I do the job properly. It is a relief to be allowed out to go and post letters. Fresh air! Birds singing! (REAL birds – not the ones on that CD.)

**QUESTION:** How am I going to survive another day like today?

**ANSWER:** I don't know. Perhaps it will get better. (Hope springs eternal.)

**Back on the train (again)**

When the train gets to Borechester, I scan the platform eagerly for a sighting of Harry, but there is no sign of him. I expect he stayed on in Borechester to do his bar work. I wonder where he works? With a sudden pang of conscience, I think about Mark instead, slaving away over a hot computer. I hope Mum and Dad have not said or done too many embarrassing things in my absence.

I look at the golden painting in my folder. Kaz has promised to look at my work tomorrow, as she ran out of time today. The golden painting was a sketch of my aura, but Kaz said it didn't capture the full majesty which surrounds me (I can't quite see it myself, although I kept looking in the mirror in the corner of the studio). So she took a few photos of my aura with a special camera just before I left, and said that she would show me the results tomorrow.

**Back home (again), in the office:**

'Hello, Alex!'

'Hello, Mark. You're still here.'

'Yes. I've finished work for the day, but I asked your dad if it was OK for me to hang on to say hello to you.'

'Oh . . . right. That's nice. Where is Dad, anyway?'

'I don't know . . .'

'Mark . . . ?'

'Yes, Alex?'

'Can you see my aura?'

'No! NO! Of course not! I wasn't looking! Really, Alex, what do you think I *am* – a total sleaze?'

'I said my *aura*, Mark.'

'Alex! You'll get me into trouble for sexual harassment in the workplace!'

'SEXUAL HARASSMENT?!!'

'Alex, shhhh!' Mark starts whistling loudly. I realise that this is a nervous reaction rather than extreme cheerfulness, but it still annoys me (I have had a hard day).

'Unsolicited whistling in the workplace is also a serious matter!' I snap, marching out of the office and narrowly avoiding a collision with Dad, who is carrying a mug of coffee. (If Mark carries on whistling, I might not feel so bad about being attracted to Harry. But I don't want to fall out with Mark.)

'Isn't Mark meant to make the coffee?' I ask.

'He's had a promotion,' Dad replies. 'I want him to concentrate on upgrading Mr Tonkin's computer, so he's excused from coffee-making. Mark really knows his stuff! And besides,' Dad whispers to me over his shoulder, 'his coffee was atrocious!' Dad looked at his watch. 'It's time Mark went home.' (I agree.)

I try to look as if I'm not bothered about anything.

'You look worried, Alex,' says Mum, joining us. 'Everything OK?'

'Fine. I'm just tired, that's all. I might go and see Abby.'


**At Abby's house, in her room**

'Alex!' Abby exclaims, throwing her arms around me. 'I am so glad to see you! Isn't Work Experience GREAT? I never realised how much FUN it would be!!!'

It suddenly seems like the wrong moment to moan about the incredibly boring day I've had, and how my love life is a total mess. (Is everyone else having a great time, apart from me? Is it something to do with ME?)

And, anyway, Abby is not in Listening Mode. Her biggest problem seems to be getting a numb bum from sitting on the tiny chairs in Class One. Then she drones on about a young male teacher at St Bart's called Colin Loveridge, with whom she has fallen head over heels in love (he doesn't know). I am saved from hearing more about the sexy way Colin Loveridge brushes back his hair with his hand by the arrival of Fabulosa, who throws herself on to Abby's bed, kicking off her expensive shoes.

'I am, as you say, POOPED!' she announces.

'So, Fabulosa,' I begin, 'is it a hectic and glamorous whirl of activity, working on *Tarte* magazine?'

'Oh, Alex! It really is!'

COLIN
LOVERIDGE

'How many famous people have you met so far?' Abby asks.

'Dozens! I can't remember!'

'And how many parties have you been to?'

'Er . . . the parties are usually at night, Alex, after I've come home. But I may get invited to one at the weekend, and maybe I can stay with Uncle Laszlo at his London flat. I don't know . . .'

'What about the chauffeur?' I enquire. 'The one who squeezes you fresh orange juice?'

'You mean Bruno? He's great. I spend a lot of time in the car with him.'

'I bet you do!'

'Yes. And also my father, he is there too.'

'What – in the car?' I ask.

'No, we put him on the roof. That is a joke, Alex! See? I am catching on to your sense of humour!'

'But you don't mean your father goes with you to work?'

'Yes. He does. It is his car and Bruno is his chauffeur, not mine. So of course he comes. Always.' I think I detect a slightly flat note in Fabulosa's usually cheerful tone of voice.

BRUNO

'Also,' Fabulosa continues, 'he likes to say hello to my cousin and make sure that I have a good time at *Tarte* and that everyone is treating me well.'

I try to imagine what it would be like if Dad came to the studio with me . . . I picture him sitting in a corner, wearing one of his dreadful beige cardigans, and waving to me every few minutes, occasionally calling out to Kaz: 'I'm just here to make sure she has a good time!' I shudder.

'But tomorrow will be a good day!' Fabulosa exclaims suddenly. 'Er . . . I mean, it will be an EVEN better day than all the other GREAT days!!!' (Why am I beginning not to believe her?)

'What's happening tomorrow?' Abby asks.

'I'm going with the Features editor to interview Brett Trousler in his beautiful London home!'

My jaw drops. (Brett Trousler is SEXEEEEE!!! And he can sing!)

'Oh – can you get his autograph for me?' I ask. 'Pleeeease?! And if he has any spare posters of himself lying around, I'd love one. Rosie drew on mine!'

'You're so lucky, Fab!' Abby exclaims. 'Meeting Brett Trousler certainly beats making folders for the children to use at school. Today I made forty-seven folders!'

Abby's mobile bleeps. It is a message from Tracey to say

that she can't join us this evening as she has to read some 'papers'.

'What papers?' Fabulosa asks.

'Probably back issues of *Tarte* magazine, knowing Tracey!' says Abby, who sounds annoyed that Tracey isn't coming.

'I don't know,' I say. 'Tracey's gone all serious recently. I prefer the old Tracey.'

BRETT TROUSLER

Fabulosa sighs. 'I miss being with all the gang at school. At least my dad isn't allowed in there.'

I glance at Fabulosa, who looks quite despondent.

'Cheer up!' I say. 'You're the lucky so-and-so who's getting to meet Brett Trousler tomorrow!'

'My dad's coming too,' she says. (I don't believe it!) 'He says he doesn't trust these pop and rock stars.

'But it will be pretty cool to meet Brett Trousler,' I say.

'With my dad there? I don't think so, Alex! I am not so keen on this Work Experience thing.'

Abby's mobile bleeps again. 'It's a message from Rowena,' she says. 'She must be having too much fun with those lifeguards at the leisure centre. Says she's sorry, but she can't make it tonight. I don't believe it! We're already losing touch with each other! I don't like this.'

'Don't panic, Abby!' I say. 'Why don't we drop in on her

one evening? She told me she's doing the late shift on Friday. And at least none of us would have to get up for work the following morning, if we went then.'

'OK. Why not?' says Fabulosa.

'I'll let Tracey know what's happening,' I say.

Abby's phone bleeps yet again. 'Message from Clare,' she says. 'Guess what? She won't be coming here this evening, because she's decided to go straight home. Says she's tired.'

'Probably wants to get her beauty sleep,' Fabulosa remarks. 'I've heard that one of the vets is quite hunky.'

'You've got that faraway look, Alex,' says Abby. 'Are you dreaming of Mark? Or is it someone else?'

'Er . . . no! NO! There's no one else! I'm just tired.'

'Come on – I can read you like a book!'

'As long as you can't see my aura.'

'Your what?' Fabulosa asks.

'Oh, yes,' says Abby. 'My mum knows about auras.'

'It's a sort of . . . er, haze around me,' I explain. 'It isn't visible to the naked eye, but you can sort of feel it if you're tuned into that sort of thing, like Kaz, and you can take photos of it with a special camera . . . and apparently mine is golden because . . . er, because . . .'

'WHO IS HE, ALEX??!'

'A boy I met on the train. He's an art student. His name's Harry.'

'Have you told Mark?'

'No! I don't need to! Harry and I are just friends. Mark and I have fallen out. He got all stressed about me getting him into trouble for sexual harassment or something, and then he started whistling . . .'

Fabulosa and Abby scream with laughter, as I do my best to explain.

## Wednesday July 3rd

### Day Three of Work Experience

**7 a.m.** As I am getting more practised at spiking my hair, there is no need to get up so early (and I need my beauty sleep). I spend more time than usual on my make-up and wonder if I will see Harry today. I never see him at Little Borehampton, the station where I catch the train, so I assume he must get on at one of the stops before me. I make sure I have my art folder with me to show Kaz. Maybe I will have a chance to show Harry too . . .

**7.45 a.m.** 'Hello, Mark.'

'Hello, Alex. I'm sorry if I got a bit stressed yesterday, but I was having alignment problems, and backing up to CD-RW can be a complete nightmare without the right software. And I've got buffer under-run problems.'

'I'm sorry to hear that.' The fact that Mark is turning into a computer nerd makes me feel better about being attracted to Harry. Surely no one could blame me for dumping a computer nerd? Well, maybe they could . . . and I'm not even sure I want to dump him.

'And I've still got to load Windows XP on to Mr Tonkin's computer,' Mark drones on. 'But it's refusing to detect the modem and now the motherboard's playing up, and I have an awful feeling there aren't enough PCI slots. Nightmare! Your dad says I'm allowed to arrive early for work as long as I wait in the kitchen and have some cornflakes or something until he's ready.'

'Right.'

'What have you done to your hair, Alex? I don't mean the spikes – but it just looks really nice. It's almost . . . golden.'

(Oh no – he's being nice again and making me like him! Time to go.)

I no longer power walk to the station. I have opted instead for an easy and confident stroll, more suited to someone who knows Who They Are and Where They Are Going. I notice that dark clouds are rolling in over the horizon and the air is humid.

### At the station

'The next train due on Platform 2 will be for Borechester, Plumbury, Spurge, Fluxham and Gorbling Sands. This train is running approximately half an hour late. This is due to necessary engineering works.'

There is a collective sigh and assorted mutterings from the usual crowd of commuters. I am going to be a few minutes late for work. Unlike Mark, I refuse to get stressed about this. As Kaz said, I have the soul of an artist. I am a free spirit, unconstrained by the narrow boundaries of time and space.

 THE NEXT TRAIN ... IS RUNNING HALF AN HOUR LATE ...

**On the train (at last)**

'Had a nasty fright, love? HARR HARR HARR!!!' I hand my ticket to the guard without bothering to look at him or say anything. He is not worth it. My mobile rings.

'You'd better turn that thing off, love,' says the guard, leaning over me. 'This is a "Say NO to Mobile Phones Zone"! People don't like it, you see? All that ringing, the whole time. Who is it – your boyfriend? HARR HARR HARR!!!'

Grabbing my folder, I squeeze past the guard and take my mobile out into the narrow corridor between the carriages.

'Hello?'

'Alex?'

'Mum!'

'You forgot your lunch.'

'Oh, bother! That means it's yak's yogurt or nothing for me. Was there anything else?'

'No, darling – I just miss you, that's all. You seem so grown up, going off to work . . .'

'OK, Mum! You'll see me later! I'd better go. Love you! Bye!'

(Parents choose strange moments to get sentimental. Perhaps she was listening to sad music, or looking through old photograph albums.)

I decide to walk a little further up the train, just in case . . . And there he is. Harry! (He has bleached his hair and is even better-looking!)

'Hello, Alex! Come and sit down.'

'Hello, Harry!'

'Your hair looks nice – almost . . . golden.'

I seem to have lost the power of speech. I just sit there, glowing. Then I manage to stammer: 'Y . . . your hair looks g . . . good too!'

'Yes, I bleached it. Mum says I look like a haystack! So you're off to your studio, are you?' Harry asks.

'Oh . . . yes.'

'I'd love to see some of your work.'

'I've got some here!'

'Let's see.'

Opening up my folder with a slightly trembling hand (this isn't too noticeable as the whole train is juddering), I spread out the contents on the table between us. Harry sifts through my drawings of our cat, a couple of self-portraits and a selection from my Abstract Period. Then he picks out Kaz's painting of my aura.

NOW – THAT'S <u>REALLY</u> GOOD!

'Now, that's *really* good! I like that!'

'Ah. Yes. I'm pleased with that one.' (Oh NO!!! I've done it again! Why did I pretend it was *my* painting? I feel awful. Then I feel angry – WHY couldn't he have chosen one of MY pictures to like?)

'It's inspired! It's beautiful! It's . . .'

'Nearly your stop,' I interrupt, feeling very uncomfortable.

My meetings with Harry are very short, and I always end up saying weird things. I really like him, and I *think* he likes me, but I wish I didn't get so nervous! It may have something to do with the image of Mark looking hurt and reproachful, which keeps popping into my mind at the wrong moment!

**At the studio**

'You're late, Alex,' says Kaz in a rather clipped voice, turning disconcertingly from Kaz into Stern Employer. 'Punctuality is important, you know.'

'Er, I'm sorry! The train . . .'

'Never mind!' She is Kaz again. 'Come and look at these photos of your aura. They came out well.'

I lean over to look. My head is apparently on fire, a golden blaze!

'Can I take one of these to show my friends?'

Kaz laughs. 'Of course! And I'll try to do a better job of painting you in all your glory! But first, help me close those windows, Alex – I think there's a storm brewing. It's quite spectacular, watching lightning through this ceiling. But I don't think we'll use the iron staircase outside the building just at the moment.' (Phew!) 'We'll use the internal stairs, I think.' (I think so too.)

'Robert Fulmington-Jarvis will be in later. He's my agent. Oh, and Nigel Farquahar, from Plumbury Fine Arts – he's coming to see us about the exhibition.'

A real live artist's agent! At last I get to interact with other people, and develop my Key Skills. Mr Chubb will be pleased. And I hope Robert will be so impressed by my work that he immediately takes me on to his books – or at least lets me use the computer.

'I don't know how much painting I'll get done today!' Kaz continues. 'Never mind . . . Put on some "Peaceful Nature Sounds", Alex – I feel in need of them . . .'

Suddenly my mobile bleeps. It is a message from Tracey: 'Trouble at work because my mobile keeps ringing. Trouble with Zak. Talk L8r.'

'Turn that thing off!' Kaz barks at me, switching into Stern Employer Mode. 'I cannot abide mobiles, and I will

NOT have them in the studio!' (This is definitely like being back at school, where the teachers hate mobiles too. There seem to be 'rules' everywhere you go, many of them depressingly similar to school rules.)

I have forgotten my walkman, so I am stuck with 'Peaceful Nature Sounds'. I wonder what's going on with Tracey . . .

ROBERT THE AGENT

Robert the Agent arrives and talks business with Kaz. He is a tall, broad-shouldered man, wearing a pinstriped suit, pink shirt with matching tie and handkerchief, and very shiny shoes.

'Robert used to be in the army,' says Kaz, after she has introduced me. 'He's very good at getting his foot through the door on other people's behalf.'

'So, you're an artist as well, are you?' Robert says to me. Things are definitely getting more interesting around here, and I no longer feel quite so depressed at the prospect of yak's yogurt for lunch and not being allowed to use my mobile.

'Show us your work, Alex!' says Kaz. 'I've been meaning to look at it, but I've been so busy preparing for the exhibition.'

I fetch my art folder and spread out the contents on a table.

'Is that your cat?' Kaz asks. 'Those are lovely drawings, Alex – you've really captured the essence of a cat. Very clever. What do you think, Robert?'

Robert is stroking his chin. 'Hmm,' he says thoughtfully. 'Hmm . . . hmm . . . hmm . . . Right. Can we get on now, Kaz? The *Plumbury Gazette* wants to do a feature on you.'

Is that it? Is that all he could say – 'Hmm'?! Even Mr Gribble, the most depressed teacher at school, has been known to show more enthusiasm than *that*.

Gloomily, I put my work away again. The prospect of yak's yogurt looms large. At least Kaz liked my cat drawings. But it looks like I will have to wait a little longer for my Big Break.

DAAAHLING!!!

NIGEL FARQUAHAR

'Daaahling!!!' A very thin man wearing a dark green velvet suit, which looks several sizes too big for him, and a light green cravat, bursts in through the door, flutters across the room to Kaz and goes 'MWAH!' loudly on both sides of her face. This must be Nigel Farquahar from Plumbury Fine Arts. He has the strangest hair I have ever seen – it is

MWAH! MWAH!

perfectly flat on top, but bushes out into a profusion of curls on either side of his face. He has a long, thin nose like a bird's beak, and stares down it at me, curling his top lip slightly.

'Kaz, darling, who is that young person, and what is she doing in your studio?'

'This is Alex, Nigel. She's doing her Work Experience in the studio. She's been such a help to me – in fact, she's my golden treasure! I'm even painting her aura. I've never seen anything like it – such radiance!'

(The foolish grin has returned to my face). Nigel sniffs loudly and turns his back on me. (Thanks for that, Nige – what did I ever do to *you*?)

'Just show Nigel your work, Alex! Come over here.' Kaz calls to me. Reluctantly, I take my art folder over to where they are standing, around the desk with the computer on it. (This has to be a mistake.) I open up my folder and Nigel flicks through the pictures inside it.

'EURGH!!!' he exclaims. (Oh, come *on*! My work isn't *that* bad.) 'Cats!' he gasps, fanning himself with his hand. 'I can't abide them! I'm allergic . . .' He sneezes loudly. (Allergic to a *picture* of a cat?! I wonder what would happen if he encountered a *real* cat.)

I feel that Nigel and I have not really hit it off. It seems unlikely that my work will now adorn the walls of Plumbury Fine Arts.

'I'll send Alex over to the gallery tomorrow afternoon, Nigel,' Kaz persists. 'I know you can always do with some extra help, and it would be a good experience for her.'

Would it? The expression on Nigel's face says no. But I expect there will be other people at the gallery – friendly ones, I hope – and it should be a lot more interesting than the usual round of washing brushes, etc.)

'By the way, Alex,' Kaz continues. 'You're on the guest list for the private view of my exhibition. I'm hoping to get the painting of your aura finished in time, so that it can be included.'

'Oh, wow! Cool.'

'I'll be sending an invitation to your family.' (AAARGH!!! The dial on the Potential Embarrassment-o-Meter has just swung around to EXTREME. Perhaps I can persuade them not to come – apart from Daniel, who *can* be cool, sometimes). 'And why don't you bring your boyfriend?'

(I just manage to stop myself saying, 'Which one?' This is going to be tricky.)

**Back on the train**
Harry gets in at Borechester! It must be his night off from bar work. I see him on the platform, about to get in two carriages along and he hasn't seen me, yet. So I quickly move to the carriage where he is about to get in, and plonk

myself down in a seat with a spare seat next to it, trying to look as if I have been there all the time.

'Harry!' I gasp, slightly out of breath. 'There's a seat here!' (There are seats everywhere.)

Harry sits next to me, and we chat about our day, and exchange mobile numbers. Things are really moving now! Unlike the train, which stops and sits in the middle of nowhere for ages. This is due to signal failure. I don't care – I want to sit here in the middle of nowhere next to Harry *for ever*!!! (I try to block out the image of Mark sitting with us, looking miserable.) Everything is going well and then I hear myself telling Harry that I have an agent called Robert. Harry laughs, but I can see from the expression on his face that he is not *quite* sure whether to believe me or not. Then I make matters worse by telling Harry that my studio is just round the corner from Plumbury Fine Arts, and the owner's name is Nigel. (I can't believe that I have just done it AGAIN! Why do I keep saying stupid things? Why am I so desperate to impress Harry? Is it because I'm worried he'll think I'm boring? I don't have this problem with Mark.)

Eventually, the train moves, slowly, and crawls into Borechester.

'See you, Harry!' I call out, as Harry gets off the train. He grins at me and waves, then turns to go.

**Walking home from the station**
There is a flash of lightning, followed by a loud rumble of

80

WHY DIDN'T MUM COME AND FETCH ME ...?

thunder. Suddenly a strong wind starts blowing and the rain comes down, lashing my face. Why didn't Mum offer to come and fetch me from the station today? I know I said I wanted to be independent – but not when it's raining. Suddenly I am aware of a car drawing up alongside me (this is all I need – a kerb crawler!). Out of the corner of my eye I notice that the car is big, black, and seems to go on for ever ... It is Fabulosa and her dad in their chauffeur-driven limousine!

'Alex! Get in! Quick!' She pushes the door open for me, and I climb into the back, and find myself sitting just behind Mr Curvetti, next to Fabulosa.

'Hello, Alex!' Mr Curvetti says, turning his head to face me. 'We will give you a lift home – the weather is not so good.'

'Oh, thanks! That's really kind!'

'Not at all! I am glad that Fabulosa has such good friends. I am bringing her home early from work today because she is so tired. Look at the big dark rings under her eyes!'

I glance at Fabulosa, who pulls a face at me. She looks very well.

'They are working the poor girl too hard at *Tarte*,' Mr Curvetti continues.

'I'm FINE, Peppi – honestly!' Fabulosa protests.

'Ah!' Mr Curvetti raises his hand, signalling that the subject is closed. 'But Father always knows best – and he knows what is best for his daughter. Is that not true, Alex?'

I grin weakly. I am not at all convinced that Dad always knows best. (If he knows best, why did he attempt to install that waste disposal unit by himself, after Mum had told him that we ought to get a plumber in? He managed to install it, but unfortunately it spewed up over a hundred gallons of rotten, stinking waste into our kitchen instead of disposing of it, and we had to get in a whole team of emergency plumbers to stop it. My brothers were fascinated, and Mum was hysterical.)

'It was so embarrassing,' Fabulosa whispers to me, 'when Peppi led me away from the *Tarte* offices by the hand! I think everyone was staring at me. Now I don't want to go back! I wish I was back at school, Alex!'

'But what about Brett Trousler?' I ask. 'Did you get to meet him?'

'No . . . When we got to his house, his agent came to the

door and told us that Mr Trousler was unavailable as he had gone internet shopping. Then she gave us signed photos of him and shut the door in our face. Here, Alex – you can have a signed photo. And here's one for Abby.'

'Oh – thanks! But that must have been so disappointing!'

'Not really. I think it was a relief, because my dad was there too, looking very angry, ready to defend me from drug-crazed rock stars!'

'Oh, Fabulosa! Ssh! Don't let your dad hear!'

Mr Curvetti turns and smiles at us benignly. The rest of the journey passes in silence and soon we arrive at my house. Mark is standing on the pavement outside my house, staring. My brothers and Rosie come spilling out through the front door, waving and pointing.

'It is nice for you to have such a welcome from your family, Alex!' Mr Curvetti exclaims. (I don't like to point out that they are only interested in the car.)

As I get out, Fabulosa calls to Mark. 'Want a lift home, Mark? Is that OK, Peppi?'

'Yes, my darling – of course we will take your charming boyfriend home!' I hear Mr Curvetti say. THE CHEEK!!! But I realise that it is not Fabulosa's fault that her dad has made this mistake, and she is making deeply apologetic gestures and faces at me through the car window.

'Er . . . I was going to stay on a bit to see you, Alex,' Mark says.

'No, no, Mark – don't worry about it! I'm sure we'll catch up soon. I should get a lift home before it tips down again.'

'OK – if you're sure?'

'Yes, Mark!'

'Bye, then!'

'Bye!'

Daniel stands beside me, and we wave goodbye as the limousine purrs away. 'So much for being independent!' he says. 'Now you've even got a chauffeur!'

'No, I haven't! It's not likely to happen again.'

'So, have you and Mark split up? Has he dumped you? Or did you dump him? Or was it a mutual thing? And is he going out with Fabulosa?'

'NO – HE IS NOT!!!' I give Daniel a hard stare. 'Couldn't you go back to just being interested in football?' I ask.

**Safe at last from Horrible Little Brothers, in my room . . .**
I remember the distressed message which Tracey sent me earlier today, so I call her to ask what the matter is.

'It's Zak,' she says. 'He's being really strange. I think we're growing apart, because of Work Experience. It's like

84

we're both not the same person – I mean, people – any longer, and it's breaking my heart.'

'Go on,' I say, soothingly but encouragingly.

'It started with him saying he didn't think he wanted to go out with me any more because I look old enough to be his mother in those clothes I wear to work . . .'

'That was a bit hard.'

'Then he said he didn't like the idea of me being surrounded by smarmy lawyers.'

'But that's your job.'

'Exactly! And I think it's just an excuse. He's trying to put the blame on *me*, but it's *him*, really. Alex – I think he's having an office romance with a glamorous estate agent.'

'Which glamorous estate agent?'

'I don't know! But there must be one.'

'I think . . .' I say, slowly, 'I think the more likely explanation is that Zak is deeply intimidated by the fact that you are a successful, high-flying career woman in a predominantly male-dominated environment.'

'What?'

'He thinks you've got a better job than he has.'

'Oh. Well, if that's all it is . . .'

'You can cope with that?'

'Yes. Poor Zak. I don't want to scare

I THINK HE'S HAVING AN OFFICE ROMANCE . . .!

him. I must try and get through to him that I can be a top lawyer *and* still be the same person. And we must learn to trust each other more, now that we're both out there in the world. Thanks, Alex!'

'It's OK.'

Artist *and* agony aunt! How do I do it? Sadly, I don't seem able to sort out my own problems quite so easily!

I end the day by using up the last of my phone credit sending a message to Abby, asking her to come round after work tomorrow, as I need someone to talk to, and it is probably not the right moment to ask Mum and Dad if I can phone Daisy. They've just received the Phone Bill From Hell, and there is much spluttering and economising in the air.

It feels strange, now that I am not seeing Abby at school every day. I feel almost . . . cut off. And I miss Daisy loads. But at least I have working at the gallery to look forward to tomorrow. I hope Nigel doesn't give me a hard time.

## Thursday July 4th

**Day Four of Work Experience**

**7.30 a.m.** I have decided to adopt a more laid back approach to life, work and everything. In other words I allowed myself an extra half-hour of SLEEP. (Need more Sleeping Experience!)

**7.50 a.m.** Not quite so laid back now. Panicking slightly, as I don't want to be late or miss my train. (My hair seems inclined to stand on end by itself, without any assistance.)

I remember to take a packed lunch today (the memory of the yak's yogurt lingers on.) and head for the front door.

Mark arrives, whistling, which puts me on edge. (How boring Mark's hair is, compared with Harry's bleached and beautiful hair!)

'Hello, Alex! Fabulosa's really nice, isn't she?'

'Yes.' (Forget it, Mark. She's out of your league. And you're supposed to be going out with me.)

'Alex . . .'

'Yes?'

'I just wanted to say . . . your dad is something else! He's amazing! There isn't *anything* he doesn't know about computers. He silenced Mr Tonkin's modem yesterday – I couldn't do it. But you should have seen how quickly he launched the Control Panel, double-clicked the Modems icon, clicked the Properties button and dragged the speaker volume slider to the left!'

'Oh, yes. I've seen him do that before.' (Help! My boyfriend has definitely turned into a computer nerd! I'm not even sure if he *is* my boyfriend any more.)

'You know something, Alex?'

'What?'

'I can see myself in the future being exactly like your dad!' Mark announces proudly.

'Wha . . . at??!'

That's IT. The ultimate turn-off! Mark and I are finished – he doesn't know it yet, but we are. No way am I going out with a boy who's threatening to turn into a clone of my dad!

'What's the matter, Alex?' Mark asks, wonderingly, as I seize my packed lunch and hare out through the door, trying to escape the nightmarish vision of Mark in a pair of thick-rimmed glasses, a beige cardigan and saying, 'Thank you, dear!' as I bring him his morning coffee and a biscuit while he tinkers around with a computer. NOOOOOO!!!

**On the train** (but only just, with seconds to spare! Why are always on time when I am late!?)

I find Harry, who is standing in the train corridor as it is so crowded today.

'Hi, Alex!'

'Hi, Harry!' (So far, so good. I have not said anything strange!)

'I'm glad to see you,' he says. (Oh, wow!) 'Did you say that your studio's just round the corner from Plumbury Fine Arts? Does it have a green door? I think I know where you are! I know Plumbury quite well . . . I was wondering if I could visit your studio tomorrow?'

'Er . . . what? I mean, I . . .'

'I've got a free day, after my first lecture. And there's a shuttle bus from Borechester to Plumbury which goes every half hour. I could be with you by eleven-thirty. You're not too busy, are you?'

'I don't think . . .'

'You don't think you are? That's good! So I won't be holding you up from anything. I won't stay too long, anyway. It's just that I've never been to a real, working art studio before, and art is what I want to do with my life. I admire the way you've already got in there, Alex – I really do! And will that agent be there tomorrow? I'm sorry if you thought I didn't believe you that he was *your* agent! It's just so . . . well, incredible!'

Before I can say anything, we have to squeeze out of the way as the steward pushes the refreshments trolley past. Harry and I are separated as a small crowd of commuters push their way to the trolley to buy coffee.

'I'll see you tomorrow, Alex!' Harry calls out. (It is nearly his stop.) 'You won't see me on the train tomorrow, because I'm staying with friends tonight. So I'll see you at the studio!'

A crowd of commuters surge past and my despairing cry, 'No, Harry! Wait!', goes unnoticed. It is too late! I will have to phone him and make some excuse. ('The studio's flooded! The ceiling's fallen in! It's too dangerous to go there! I'm emigrating!') Or I could just tell him the truth . . . But when I reach into my pocket for the piece of paper with

Harry's phone number on it, I find, to my horror, that it has got wet (probably from yesterday's rain, as I was soaked before Fabulosa offered me the lift), and the ink has run, making it illegible.

DOOM!!!

**At the studio** (I arrive with a sinking feeling, my hair standing on end more than ever).

'Ah, there you are, Alex!' says Kaz. 'I'm glad you're here, because there's lots to do, especially since I won't be here tomorrow.'

'You won't?' (I am trying not to sound too hopeful.)

'No. I'd still like you to come, though. Answer the phone, sweep up – that sort of thing. Looking after the studio will be your responsibility in my absence, but I'll leave Robert's number with you, just in case. He'll be at the gallery, and I'll show you where that is later. Robert will come straight over, if you need anything. Aurelia will be here to let you in tomorrow and she knows what to do if you need any help – so you won't be completely on your own. But Orion and I are off to an Indian Clapping Sounds workshop.'

'Indian Clapping Sounds?'

'Yes. I don't know if you've noticed, but Orion is terribly tense. His energy is trapped. There are hard knots of energy clustered throughout his body.'

**ORION IS TERRIBLY TENSE**

'Oh.'

90

It is nothing compared with how I am feeling at the moment! WHY do I get myself into these situations?! I may be able to get away with it – this time – if Kaz isn't there when Harry comes to visit. But I must tell him the truth! I know that's what Daisy and Abby would both say.

'What are Indian Clapping Sounds?' I ask, trying to sound calm and in control. I want Kaz to feel confident that she can safely leave me in charge!

'Indian Clapping Sounds release the energy!' Kaz explains. 'They arise out of the body's own natural biorhythms, and lead to perfect synchronisation and re-alignment of the Tchi. They also calm the mind, and have been said to have a beneficial effect on every organ in the body.'

'Great!'

'So that's where Orion and I are going tomorrow. It's the Advanced Indian Clapping Sounds workshop. Will you be all right her on your own, Alex?'

'No problem! I'll be fine on my own.'

'Thank you, Alex. Let's get on with things now – make me a cup of Heavenly Herbal, will you? Later I'll take you round to the gallery.'

INDIAN CLAPPING SOUNDS
RELEASE THE ENERGY!

**At the gallery**

'DAAAAAHLING!!!' (Oh no). 'MWAH! MWAH!' Nigel embraces Kaz. I quickly sidestep behind a large bronze sculpture shaped like an egg. (This must be where the sculptures in Kaz's garden come from. They are by another artist, whose name I don't recognise.) Nigel frowns in my direction. Luckily the phone rings.

'Answer it!' he shouts at a girl who is seated at a desk halfway down the gallery. She has bright pink cropped hair and is wearing thick black eyeliner, a dress apparently made out of a bin-liner fastened with safety pins, and a permanent scowl. Unwillingly, she extends a hand with talon-like fuchsia pink fingernails and picks up the receiver.

'Plumbury Fine Arse?' she says.

'ARTS!!!' screams Nigel. 'It's Plumbury Fine Arts! I don't know WHY we employ that girl! I swear she loses me customers every day! But what can I do? Why does she have to be the daughter of one of our most generous patrons?'

'Call for you, Nige!' says the girl, holding the phone out to Nigel, and staring at him balefully.

'Don't call me Nige, Bianca! You should address me as Mr Farquahar!'

'Yes, Mr Farter.'

Seething, Nigel grabs the receiver roughly from Bianca's hand ('Ow! Mind my nails!'), and shouts, 'Yes?'

There is an indistinct babble on the other end of the

92

phone, and Nigel's whole attitude visibly changes. He half cringes, and a sickly smile spreads across his face.

BIANCA

'Of *course*, Mr Cussington-Wilberforce,' he intones in an oily voice, 'your bronze of the prancing stallion will be ready for collection at your earliest convenience.'

As soon as Nigel has finished on the phone, Kaz turns to me. 'I've got to go and get on with my work, Alex – I'm sure Nigel will find you plenty to do.'

After she has gone, Nigel hands me a box full of paper clips. 'SOMEONE,' he says, glaring at Bianca, who scowls back, 'made these paper clips into a long chain! I want them taken apart again. Can you do that?' he asks me.

I nod. (This is going to be exciting. *Not*.)

'I'm going upstairs for a while to lie down,' Nigel announces. 'I am utterly stressed. Call me if we have a customer.'

The afternoon passes quietly. The gallery is not exactly a buzzing hive of activity. Bianca doesn't say very much, and spends most of the time doing her nails. It is a relief when Nigel decides to close the gallery for the day and I am sent back to the studio.

'You must be tired, Alex,' says Kaz, sympathetically. 'I

expect Nigel worked you hard. You'd better go home and get some rest.'

**Going home** (no Harry . . . no hope of getting out of tomorrow!)

I reflect that Work Experience is giving me a good idea of what I don't want to do. I don't want to work at a gallery! At least, not at Plumbury Fine Arse.

**Back home**

Mark has gone, but Abby arrives soon afterwards, looking upset.

'What's up, Abby? You look as though you might have knots of trapped energy throughout your body. I guess your biorhythms need synchronising. Kaz recommends Indian Clapping Sounds.'

Abby doesn't even smile.

'Oh dear – there really *is* something the matter, isn't there?'

'Yes.'

'Come and tell me about it.'

We sit on the bed in my room and I put my arm around her.

'It's so awful, Alex. I don't know what to do. I can't go back to St Bart's.'

'Why not?'

'I just *can't*! That's all!'

'Abby! Explain, please! It can't be *that* bad. Can it?'

THEY WERE BEING MEAN TO ROSIE ...

'Yes.'

'So what's happened?'

'Rosie took Yellow Bunny to school . . .' Abby begins.

'Oh, right! Look, Abby, I know Yellow Bunny's pretty disgusting – I mean, you just don't know where it's *been*, do you? But I don't think you should give up your job because of it. Perhaps you could have some counselling to help you overcome your phobia of yellow bunnies . . .'

'No, no, no! You don't understand! Just listen, will you?'

'OK. I'm listening.'

'These two girls from one of the older classes got hold of Yellow Bunny, and they were throwing it around the playground and being really mean to Rosie, saying she was a stupid little baby with a smelly little bunny. And then Rosie started crying. I couldn't just stand there and do nothing. So I got Yellow Bunny back and told the two girls to stop being horrible and to go and say sorry to Rosie.'

YELLOW BUNNY

'Did they?'

'Yes.'

'Well, it sounds like you handled that situation really well. What's the problem?'

'At the end of school, I went out into the playground and everyone was looking at me and giggling.'

'Why?'

'Those two girls had written, in chalk, "Miss Abby luvs Mr Loveridge" in huge letters, right across the playground.'

'But how did they know?'

'I don't *know*! Children. . . they notice things. Maybe they saw the way I looked at him, or something. I don't know . . . But Alex, it was so awful! Some parents were looking at it, and the two other people doing Work Experience at the school – I don't know them very well – were grinning, and then . . .'

Abby seems to be struggling to say something so hideously awful that the words are sticking in her throat.

Miss Abby
Luvs
Mr Loveridge

'What happened?' I ask softly.

96

'*He* – Colin Loveridge – came out and . . . and he looked at it! I just ran! And I'm NEVER going back!!!' Abby bursts into tears.

'Oh . . . Abby! Don't cry!' I stroke her hair.

Suddenly I notice Rosie standing in the doorway.

'Why is Miss Abby crying, Alex?'

'Oh, Rosie!' exclaims Abby. 'I'm not Miss Abby – just Abby, that's all! Come here and let me give you a hug!'

Abby puts her arms around Rosie, who is looking very solemn.

'Rosie . . .' says Abby, making an effort to stop crying.

'Yes, Miss . . . yes, Abby?'

'Would you be very sad if I didn't come back to St Bart's?'

Now it is Rosie's turn to burst into loud sobs.

'I think that means yes, she would be *very* sad,' I remark.

'You MUST come back!' says Rosie, between sobs. 'If you don't come back, Jonathan will cry. And you mustn't make Jonathan cry, because he's my best friend!'

'OK, Rosie,' sniffs Abby. 'I will come back – just for you. And Jonathan. And I suppose they need *someone* to make all those folders.'

'Oh, good!' says Rosie. 'I'll stay with you *all* day, Abby, and I'll hold your hand, and I'll make sure *no* one's nasty to you!'

'Thank you, Rosie! You're the best!'

'So are you, Abby. You're the best too!'

'OK, OK!' I interject. 'Sorry to break up the Mutual Admiration Society and all that, but it's time Rosie went to bed.'

Abby gives Rosie a kiss. I can't help reflecting that Abby would soon change her attitude if she had to put up with a little sister full-time, borrowing her make-up without asking, demanding Mum's attention the *whole* time . . . but never mind.

'Rosie . . .' I say, just as Rosie is about to leave.

'Yes, Alex?'

'Don't take Yellow Bunny to school again.'

'OK.' Suddenly a huge grin lights up Rosie's face. 'This is all Yellow Bunny's fault, isn't it? He's a *naughty* bunny!'

'Yes, Rosie. Yellow Bunny is a *very* naughty bunny!'

After Rosie has left, I tell Abby all about Harry and the impending visit to the studio.

'Wow! Alex! You certainly get into some weird situations! I hope for your sake nothing goes wrong. Isn't it better to be honest? And I don't suppose you've told poor Mark? All this is going on behind his back.'

'I *wish* everyone would stop calling him "poor Mark"! In case you haven't noticed, Mark is *very* happy surrounded by computers. He's getting on like a house on fire with Dad. Mark's OK.'

'Hmm. I'm glad you think so. Anyway, thanks for listening to me this evening. Rosie's lovely.'

'So am I!'

'Yes, Alex – you're lovely too. But I'm not looking forward to tomorrow.'

'Will you message me? Or call? Let me know how it goes? I'm sure everything will work out.'

I am *not* sure that things are going to work out for me!

## Friday July 5th

**Day Five of Work Experience! – end of Week One**

**7.30 a.m.** I bash the alarm clock with the flat of my hand and send everything flying off the bedside table. Another alarm clock goes off on a nearby shelf and I hurl it across the room. I guess the novelty of the working life is beginning to wear off . . . I just want to SLEEEEEP!!! And I HATE TRAINS!!!! I haven't slept well and I am in a bad mood. I know I am going to have to tell Harry the truth – that it is not *my* studio, and that I don't have an agent, and that I'm just doing Work Experience. I feel nervous about this, and I am very worried that Harry won't like me when he finds out that I have not told the whole truth (in other words, that I lied). How can I expect anyone to understand that stupid things come out of my mouth when I'm nervous? I also feel bad about Mark, especially after what Abby said about going behind his back. Am I really doing that?

**7.55 a.m.** 'Sorry, Mark – I can't stop. I'm late . . . I'm stressed. Goodbye!'

**8.20 a.m.** I leap on to the train just as the doors are closing.

'Running a bit late, are we, love?' The guard guffaws. 'Stayed up too late chatting to our boyfriend on our mobile, did we?'

'Maybe you did!' I shout at him. 'But that's your own business! Nothing to do with me!'

'Ooooooh!' exclaims the guard, looking shocked. 'You're so sharp, you'll cut yourself, missy!'

I squash myself into a corner seat and lean my head against the window. I close my eyes. Why am I getting so stressed? Everything's going to be FINE. Yes, it is. But I keep remembering Abby's words: 'I hope for your sake nothing goes wrong . . .' (Just the sort of thing Daisy would have said!) I get even more nervous because there is no sign of Harry – then I remember that he stayed in Borechester last night. (I must stop panicking!!!)

OOOOOOH!

I AM STRESSED ...

**8.50 a.m.** My mobile rings.

'Oi!' bellows the guard so loudly that all the other commuters jump. 'I thought I told you to turn that thing off!'

I scurry out into the corridor. 'Hello?'

'Alex? It's Abby.'

'Abby! Are you OK?'

'Everything's fine. The two girls' parents were told about their daughters' graffiti in the playground, and they've just been in with the girls to see the headmaster. I was asked to go into his office while they were there, and they had to say they were sorry to me. And they looked so little and scared, I couldn't go on being angry.'

'What about the teacher you fancy?'

'He was very nice about it – he just laughed!'

'He laughed at you?!'

'No, no! He laughed in a *nice* way, and made the whole thing seem like no big deal. He's getting married soon. He invited me to the wedding!'

'That was nice.'

'Yes. A shame that he's getting married, but nice of him to invite me. I'd better go – school's about to start.'

'Yes – and I've got to get off the train.'

'Oh, and Alex?'

'Yes?'

'Thanks for being there last night!'

'That's OK. Bye!'

I'm glad that Abby is OK. Once again I seem to be better at sorting out other people's lives than my own.

**At work**

Aurelia lets me into the studio.

'Mum said help yourself to yak's yogurt. It's in the fridge.'

'Thanks, Aurelia.'

'I've got loads of work to do. I'm writing a book on Tibet. So I'll leave you to it. You'll be OK?'

'Fine! Thanks!'

'Just shout if you want anything.'

'Thanks!' (I have decided that Aurelia is OK – better than her drippy brother, anyway.)

I try to keep myself busy, but there is only so much sweeping I can do. I suppose I could defrost the fridge . . .

The minutes tick by slowly. I wander around and look at the large painting on the easel. Kaz is still working on it. It is a larger version of the sketch she did of my aura, and it is certainly very splendid – a great swirling mass of gold, and, in the middle of the canvas I can just about make out a girl's face. She has red spikes on her head. I feel so proud to be the subject of a painting by a famous artist . . . I try to lose myself in the painting as the hands on the clock creep around to eleven-thirty . . .

'Hello.'

'AAAAARGH!!!'

'Alex?'

'Harry! D . . . Don't creep up on me like that! How did you get in?'

'Through the door. There was a girl and she just pointed me up the stairs, so in I came. Sorry I startled you.'

'That's OK! I'm glad you're here.'

'So this is your studio?'

I open my mouth to explain, but no words come out. It is so nice being admired by Harry – especially since no one else seems interested in me – Kaz seems to think the only things I'm any good at are sweeping floors and making tea.

'And is this what you're working on at the moment?' Harry peers closely at the large painting of my aura.

'Yes, that's right.' (Oh *no*! I didn't mean for it to go this far! But how do I back out now without losing face – and without losing Harry?)

'Is it a self-portrait? It looks a bit like your face in the middle.'

'Yes. That's me.'

'It's a wonderful painting. You're very talented. And this is a wonderful studio. I love the see-through ceiling! But how did you get started? You must have started very . . . er, young?'

'Yes, I did. Er, Harry . . . there's something . . .'

But Harry isn't listening. 'I want to know,' he says, 'how did your work get known? You said you have an agent?'

'I know I said that, but . . .'

'Can I meet him?'

'Maybe. I don't know. Harry . . .'

My voice trails away as Harry wanders around the studio, looking at paintings, opening drawers, peering into cupboards. He even looks in the fridge. 'You don't mind me looking around, do you?' he asks.

I shake my head. Perhaps he will leave soon and never come back. But I *want* to see him again. I don't want him to hate me! And he'll hate me if I tell him I lied. (Maybe not quite as much as I hate myself for being so STUPID!!!)

'You can carry on with your painting, if you like.'

'No, it's break-time. I mean, er, I'm taking a break! I've got artist's cramp!'

The studio telephone rings. To my horror, Harry answers it.

'Hello? Who? No, I don't think so . . . Alex, is there anyone called Kaz here?'

'No!'

'No, she's not here . . . OK, so you'll phone again later? Right. Bye!'

Harry turns to me. 'Who's Kaz?'

'Er . . . she's the cleaning lady!'

'That was her agent.'

'Ah . . .' (I am not sure how to get out of this one.)

'Alex . . . ?'

HELLO?

TO MY HORROR,
HARRY ANSWERS THE PHONE . . .

104

'Yes, Harry?' (Uh-oh. Here we go. I suppose it's for the best if he's guessed the truth.)

'I can't really stay very long today. Any chance of me coming back next week? I have quite a lot of free time on Monday and Tuesday, and term ends on Wednesday.'

'Um . . . I'm not sure . . . I'll have to get back to you on that one. Can you leave it with me?' My heart is beating like a sledgehammer. I feel too ill to confess all right now.

'That's cool,' he says. 'But Alex . . . ?'

'Yes, Harry?' (What now??! He is making me VERY nervous!!!)

'You know I like you?' (Oh, wow!)

'Yes. I mean – er, do you?'

'Yes, I do. I like you. But I'm worried.'

'Why?' (WHY is he worried? Can't we just like each other without worrying? Is he worried because he's guessed I haven't been telling the truth? Don't do this to me, Harry!)

'It's a bit hard to say . . .' (PLEEEASE try!!!) 'It's like this . . .'

'Yes?'

'You're a real artist, Alex, and I'm . . . I'm just an art student. Do you see?'

'Oh. Is that . . . sort of . . . intimidating or something?'

'Well, I wouldn't put it *quite* like that. But you've got your own studio, and your work sells. I'm just a poor student.'

'But . . . but I'm just an ordinary person, really! I go on the train! I'm really normal!'

'No, Alex. You're not. Just look at all this.' He waves his hand at the studio. 'And your amazing paintings – they're incredible.'

'Harry, I've got something to tell you . . .'

'Sorry, Alex – I've got to go and see one of my lecturers. Perhaps we can talk about this another time? I've really got to go. Thanks for inviting me here today – it's wonderful!'

'Harry! Er . . . I'm sorry, but . . . but I've lost your mobile number!'

'Oh, that's OK! Here – I'll write it on your hand.'

This makes me go all gooey, and I am unable to say anything else apart from 'Bye!'.

Harry leaves and I feel very alone. I can't phone my friends, because they aren't allowed to use their mobiles while at work. I feel tempted to use the studio phone to call Daisy, and then I remember that she will be at work, and I would probably get into trouble for using the studio phone. I feel utterly stupid for not telling Harry the truth when I had the chance . . . not that he gave me much of a chance . . . and now I've made things worse . . . And the worst thing is knowing that he'd like me a whole lot more if I hadn't said I was a famous artist!

I decide to defrost the fridge. While I am doing this, I reflect on the fact that I can always go back to Mark if it all goes wrong with Harry. Then I feel awful for thinking about Mark in this way – he deserves better, even if he whistles and talks about computers all the time! Life is SOOOOO complicated!!!

## Halfway through the afternoon

Kaz arrives back.

'Alex! How good of you to defrost the fridge! But you left the yak's yogurt sitting out. It's probably gone rancid. I may have to throw it away.' (Shame.)

'Never mind. Nothing can disturb me today,' says Kaz. 'I am full of Indian Clapping Sounds and my biorhythms are properly synchronised.'

'Brilliant!'

'Yes – and what's more, I think Orion really benefited today. It took nearly all day, but by the end of the workshop he was beginning to clap in time with the rest of us. And we got rid of nearly sixty hard knots of energy in his body. Each person clapped in turn close to his head until the bad energy was driven away. But the poor boy's exhausted – he's gone to lie down. Said he had a headache.'

'All clapped out, I should think!' I exclaim, without thinking.

Kaz looks at me, and I pretend to have a severe coughing fit.

'Go and get a glass of water, Alex! Anyway, the Indian Clapping Sounds were such a success that we're going back on Monday.'

'You are?' I say, recovering suddenly from my coughing fit.

ZAHREENA – THE BIG
CHIEF CLAPPER ( DEMONSTRATING
AN ADVANCED INDIAN
CLAPPING SOUND)

'Yes. The Workshop was so good that Zahreena – she's the Big Chief Clapper – has decided to hold an extra workshop on Monday. I expect Robert and Nigel will be cross with me, because there's still a lot to do for the exhibition, but I must put Orion's health and biorhythms first. Would you mind very much being here on your own again on Monday?'

'Oh . . . yes – I mean, I'm sure it will be fine!' (I can't believe that I am actually tempted to invite Harry to visit the studio again, but I am. Perhaps I'll tell him the truth this time . . . I WILL tell him the truth this time! It's just a matter of finding the right moment.)

The phone rings and Kaz answers it. (I tried to get to the phone first, in order to develop one of my Key Skills – using the phone – but I wasn't quick enough.)

'That was Robert, Alex,' says Kaz. 'He was concerned because someone he didn't know answered the phone when he rang earlier. He actually came round, but Aurelia told him that it was a friend, and there was nothing to worry about, so he went away again as he had a lot of work to do.' (I have decided that I really like Aurelia.) 'I don't mind, but Health and Safety Regulations state that I must always know who is on the premises, in case anything happens, so your friend should be signed in. Here – this is the Visitors' Book, Alex. Make sure they sign this and fill in the time they arrive and leave. And don't let anyone in whom you don't know. Phone Robert at once if you're at all concerned. Remember that the studio has CCTV . . .'

(This is a worrying thought. I must remember not to pick my nose, scratch my bum, etc.)

'. . . And in case of emergency,' Kaz continues, 'press this button next to the door. It will sound an alarm at the local police station. Aurelia and Orion already know not to let strangers in, but Aurelia must have realised the boy who visited was a friend of yours – is he the one you are in love with?' I feel myself blushing furiously.

'Whoever it is, Alex,' Kaz continues, 'you MUST tell me when someone is coming to the studio – all the paintings I'm working on here are irreplaceable, and some of my materials as well. And please don't allow your friend to touch anything, Alex. It's your responsibility to make sure they behave. I should have made all this clearer before.'

'It's OK. I understand. And I'm sorry. Would you mind if I had a friend here on Monday?'

'Well,' says Kaz slowly. 'I suppose it would be company for you. As long as you remember everything

I've just told you. This is a chance to prove how responsible you are.'

**Going home on the train**

After a short wrestling match with my conscience (I manage to convince myself that I can be responsible for the studio *and* have Harry there), I send a message to Harry (luckily Mum bought me some phone credit so that I can call her if there is an emergency) asking him if he can come to the studio on Monday. He sends a message back to say he can. (YESSS!)

**Back home**

So that's it. Week One of Work Experience is over. I'm exhausted. There are no signs (yet) of anyone spotting my talent and turning me into a full-time artist so that I don't have to go back to school.

It's so depressing that the most challenging task I have been given so far is to disentangle paper clips. Isn't it a well-known fact that women and girls can MULTI-TASK?! Given the chance, I could easily answer the phone, do work on the computer, talk to agents AND disentangle paper clips, all at the same time. Then I wouldn't be so bored or feel that I'm wasting my time and talent. (If I have talent, that is. I *thought* I had until this week.) But there's still a week to go . . .

I haven't spoken to Clare for ages, so I send a message: 'R U coming 2 the leisure centre?' After a while I get a reply: 'Not 2night. Washing hair. C U soon.'

I phone Abby. 'Have you heard from Clare recently?' I ask her.

'No. I've talked to her on the phone and I've asked her to come over, but she always says she's going home to have a bath or wash her hair.'

'There must be someone she's trying to impress!' I remark.

'Yes – knowing Clare, there is! Perhaps she's going out with a handsome vet!'

'Probably. Are you going to the leisure centre to see Rowena this evening?'

'Yes, I'm going now. There's a bus in ten minutes. Shall I come over, and we can go together?'

'Yes, I want to tell you about today.'

**On the bus**

I tell Abby about Harry's visit to the studio. Abby giggles.

'Honestly, Alex! You *must* tell him the truth!'

'I'm going to! Definitely!'

'It's always best to tell the truth.'

'I KNOW! Could you please stop being a teacher?' I plead.

'I'm not being a teacher – I'm being your friend. But I think I'm going to be a good teacher . . . one that the children like, I hope! And I'm very good at making folders! I'm working in a different class next week, so I won't see quite so much of Rosie. You're so lucky, having a little sister like her. I love little children.'

'And they love you. It must be nice, knowing what you want to do with your life.'

'Yes, but before that, I can't wait to get back to normal! You and me and the rest of the gang – at school together! I'm going to make the most of the time we've got left, because I know I'm going to miss it! You *are* coming back, Alex, aren't you?' Abby asks, anxiously.

'Yes! I miss you too – and I don't really know what I want to do yet. I don't think I'm going to become a successful artist overnight. I just know that I don't want to do anything that involves paper clips . . . Here's our stop . . .'

**At the leisure centre**
Tracey and Fabulosa are already there, standing by the front desk, but they look worried. (They also look as though they have gone to some trouble with their hair and make-up in order to impress the hunky lifeguards.)

'What's up?' I ask.

'It was only a joke,' says Tracey. 'We were only having fun.'

'We didn't mean to get her into trouble,' adds Fabulosa.

'Trouble? What's happened?'

'We – that's Fabulosa, Rowena and me –' Tracey begins, 'We were eyeing up one of the lifeguards. Rowena told us she thought he fancied her, because he's been really friendly to her all week. So then we followed him around while he was working, sorting out some badminton

A SHUTTLECOCK DOWN THE SHORTS
SITUATION

equipment. And I dared Rowena to . . . to . . .'

'To *what*, Tracey?'

'To stuff a shuttlecock down his shorts.'

'And she did?'

'Yes. And then he got really stressed and shouted at her, and the supervisor came over, wanting to know what was going on . . .'

'And he accused Rowena of sexual harassment!' Fabulosa continues. 'So the supervisor told Rowena to go to his office as he wanted to talk to her . . .'

'And they've been in there for about ten minutes!' Tracey finishes.

At this moment a door marked 'Office: Leisure Centre Personnel Only' opens, and a pale, subdued-looking Rowena emerges.

'Rowena! I'm so sorry!' Tracey apologises, looking close to tears herself. 'What did he say?'

'He let me off this time,' Rowena replies quietly. 'I've got to find Scott – that's the lifeguard I upset – and apologise. If he accepts my apology, then the matter is closed.'

'And if he doesn't . . . ?'

'Then I won't be allowed back next week.'

'Oh, Rowena!' Tracey exclaims. 'Let's go and find Scott now. I'll tell him it was all my fault – I put you up to it!'

We find Scott sorting out a store cupboard. He seems to have calmed down and accepts Rowena's (and Tracey's) apology.

'No worries,' he says. 'Just don't do it again. You're here to work, you know – not fool around with your mates.'

'Thanks, Scott.'

We creep away quietly, and Rowena, who is obviously relieved, shows us some of the things she's been doing.

'. . . And on Tuesday I re-stocked the vending machine,' she says.

'That's really great, Rowena!' (We all want to cheer her up and make her feel better.)

'And I've decided I'm going to train as a lifeguard and do a first aid course, and get all my certificates,' she continues. 'I really want to go to sports college. So I'm going to stay on at school until then. And I can't afford to risk all that by fooling around and upsetting people.'

'Point taken,' says Tracey.

After a while, Mr Curvetti arrives with Bruno in the limousine, and we have a lift home.

'It gives me great joy to see Fabulosa with all her nice friends!' says Mr Curvetti. We all smile, apart from Fabulosa, who looks embarrassed.

Before saying goodbye, I ask my friends if they'd like to meet up in Borechester tomorrow afternoon. Rowena says she can't, because she is going One Day Eventing. Fabulosa says she can't, as she is going to a party. But Abby says that her mum will be able to give Abby, Tracey and me a lift into Borechester if we come to her house after lunch tomorrow. We agree to try to persuade Clare to get a lift in as well and meet us. Then we say goodbye.

After I have raided the fridge (it needs de-frosting – I should remind Mum to do it), I quickly check behind the door in the office, under desks, etc., to make sure Mark is not lurking anywhere, ready to leap out and explain core XP technology to me. I am not sure that I could easily look him in the eyes at the moment . . . When I feel reassured that he has gone home for the weekend, I drag myself upstairs and have a long, relaxing bath before collapsing into bed . . . ZZZZZZZZZZ . . .

## Saturday July 6th

### Day One of the weekend
ZZZZZZZZZZZZZZZZZZZZZZZ . . . . . .

I laze around until one o'clock and send a message to Abby, asking if we are going to Borechester. She sends a message back to say that we are, and I should get round to her house as soon as possible.

'Alex!' Mum calls out to me. 'You've had a good sleep! I expect you've had a busy week with Kaz. We haven't seen much of you . . .'

'I'll catch up with you later, Mum – I've got to go now!'

'I wanted you to tidy your room, Alex, and help me sort out your clothes, and I was wondering if you'd help me defrost the fridge? And we could make chocolate brownies together! And you need to phone Aunt Primula and thank her for the "Good Luck With Your Work Experience" card, and . . .'

'OK! OK! I'll do all that later. Promise!' (Mum is the World's Leading Exponent of Multi-tasking.)

'Hi, Alex!' says Daniel, appearing at the bottom of the stairs. 'How are things between you and Mark? Anything I should know about?'

(This is getting ANNOYING!) 'NO, Daniel! Believe me – there is NOTHING you should know about! Why don't you go and tidy your room, defrost the fridge and make chocolate brownies? Oh, I forgot – boys can't multi-task. I know you have difficulty walking and talking at the same time! . . . Aaargh! Mind my hair!' In order to get out of the house, I have to get past Daniel, who is beating me over the head with a cushion, much to Rosie's delight. Finally I escape.

Tracey is already at Abby's house, and she and I get into the back of Abby's mum's car. Abby sits in front.

CLARE THINKS SHE MIGHT HAVE CAUGHT A
COLD FROM A RABBIT...

'Clare said she might meet us later,' says Abby. 'But she thinks she might have caught a cold from a rabbit because it sneezed on her.'

'What?'

'And she says she's got itchy spots on the back of her hands, and she's worried she's caught an infection from a fish, because she had to put her hand in its bowl when she was cleaning it, and . . .'

'Is Clare all right?'

'I think so.'

'Did she mention any handsome vets?'

'No.'

'But I think there's *something* going on, isn't there? Because we never see her, and she's always making excuses about washing her hair.'

'Yes, there's definitely *something* going on . . .'

'Something fishy.'

Abby's mum drops us off and arranges to meet us later.

'I'm going to learn to drive soon,' I announce. 'I'm fed up

with having to walk, and getting soaked to the skin, and I'm fed up with trains, and stupid guards who make stupid comments. And the train's always late, except when *I'm* late, and then it's on time, and . . .'

'Alex, look! – there's Mark.'

'Oh . . . er . . . Mark?'

'Yes, Alex – your boyfriend! Remember?' Abby says.

'You won't say anything about . . . ?' I whisper to Abby.

'NO, Alex!' Abby whispers back. 'What do you think I am? I won't say anything about anything as long as you promise to get it sorted out.'

'What are you two whispering about?' Tracey asks.

'Oh, nothing!'

'Let's get Mark to come and join us, and then we'll all go and visit James at the White Hart Hotel.'

'You mean James is still working?' I ask. 'At the weekend?'

'Yes. One of the other people who works there asked James to come back on Saturday – today – and help him. He just asked as a favour, and James likes him, so he said yes.'

Mark is gazing at the window display of a computer shop, drooling.

'Hello, Mark.'

'Oh! Alex! Hello. Take a look at that Sinistron Intertainment Centre with Pentium III 800 MHz, 128MB RAM, 20 EB hard drive, 3.5 inch floppy drive, DVD drive, Internal modem and networking card. And that wonderful

LCD flatscreen! Isn't it the most magnificent thing you've ever seen?'

'It's OK. We're just off to see James at the White Hart. Want to come?'

'Yes! Excellent idea! I haven't seen James all week – haven't even spoken to him. Hasn't this week just flown by? Work Experience is GREAT! Thanks to your dad, of course. I feel so incredibly focused. I've nearly finished upgrading Mr Tonkin's computer. I just need to master the interface socket and reconfigure the perniculator, and it'll be ready! I'm thinking of starting my own company called Computers to Go! If your dad would offer me a real apprenticeship, I might not go back to school.'

'Mark . . .'

'I've been building a computer in my room at night, complete with external modem, motherboard *and* father-board, masses of PCI slots, Va-Va-Voom speakers, CD-ROM drive, cordless mouse and a little external grey box with flashing green lights, which doesn't actually do anything, but it looks good.'

'MARK!'

'Yes, Alex?'

'Nothing – it doesn't matter.'

'I like that checked shirt your dad wears, Alex,' Mark continues, unabashed. 'I thought I might look for one like it.'

(I am getting the dreadful, sinking sensation again . . .)

'We could look at some anoraks later,' Tracey suggests. 'Or how about a nice pair of slippers?'

Fortunately, we have reached the White Hart Hotel, the entrance to which is through a revolving glass door, divided up into three sections, like segments of an orange. I squash into one section with Abby, and Mark is behind us. Tracey gives the door an extremely hard push and we go spinning around, several times, running fast and shrieking with laughter. Then the door shoots us out into the hotel lobby. Abby trips over and falls, and Mark and I pile into her, giggling uncontrollably.

'Don't look now!' says Tracey in a low voice. She is standing beside us, apparently fascinated by a large flower arrange-ment on a highly polished table next to a wide staircase.

'Oh dear!' says Mark quietly. He jumps to his feet and becomes equally interested in the flower arrangement.

'What?' I ask, getting to my feet and helping Abby up. Looking around, I see that there are tables and chairs dotted around the lobby, where people are sitting, drinking coffee or tea and reading newspapers or chatting. Then I understand why my friends are behaving so strangely.

Mr Chubb is sitting at a table nearby, with Mrs Chubb and the two little Chubbs. The little Chubbs are drinking milkshakes, and the whole family is staring at us. Mr Chubb gets up and walks towards us.

'Uh-oh.'

'Shall we run?' Tracey whispers.

'No! That'll make it worse!' I hiss. 'Smile! Look normal!'

We all smile cheesily at Mr Chubb.

WE ALL SMILE CHEESILY...

'Hello, Sir!'

'Hello, Alex, Mark, Tracey, Abigail. That was outstandingly stupid, what you just did, wasn't it? And dangerous – you could have knocked someone over or even caused a serious injury.'

'I know – we're sorry, Sir.'

'We won't do it again.'

Now the hotel manager has walked over to join us. (This is fun! Quite a get-together!)

'Excuse me, Sir,' says the manager. 'But are these, er . . . young people . . . your children?'

'No,' Mr Chubb replies. 'These are my children.'

He points at the little Chubbs, who both smile and wave. 'Toby and Henrietta Chubb.' Mr Chubb smiles at them and waves back, going all misty-eyed. (I am beginning to realise that Mr Chubb is a very emotional man.)

'So these young people,' (the manager indicates us with his hand), 'are nothing to do with you.'

OH, MR CHUBB!

'I'm their teacher.'

Suddenly Mr Chubb produces a large handkerchief from his pocket and buries his face in it.

'Oh, Mr Chubb!' I exclaim. 'Please don't! I'm so sorry if we upset you! We'll behave in future, really we will . . .'

'No . . . no!' snuffles Mr Chubb into his handkerchief. 'The flowers!' He points at the large flower arrangement. 'Hay fever! . . . allergic . . . that's all . . .' He shuffles off to join his family, blowing his nose loudly.

'May I ask the purpose of your visit to my hotel?' the manager demands, turning to face us. 'If it is merely to play with the revolving door, thereby putting other guests at risk, I would ask you to leave immediately. In an orderly manner.'

'Er . . . we've come to see James,' says Abby.

'James? Oh . . . yes, James. You are referring to the youth doing his Work Experience at this establishment. I am afraid he is not here today. It is the weekend.'

'Yes, we know. But he told us he was coming in today to help out a friend of his who also works here.'

'Really?' The manager raises an eyebrow. 'Such keenness. Now that's the sort of staff I want.'

We all grin cheesily again.

'Carly, have you seen the boy, James?' the manager asks a waitress, who is passing by, carrying a tray of glasses.

'Oh, yes, Mr DeVille – he's helping Harry in the bar.'

'Oh – but that is highly irregular!' exclaims Mr DeVille. 'James should not be working in the bar area. He is a youth. Youths are not allowed.'

'Well, he's not actually serving drinks, Mr DeVille . . .'

'I should think NOT!'

'He's only polishing glasses. Lending Harry a helping hand, I think.'

'Hmm. I must have a word with Harry.'

The manager strides off in the direction of the bar area.

'Let's follow him!' says Mark, and he sets off with Tracey and Abby. 'Come on, Alex!'

I am rooted to the spot. It must be the same Harry . . . Harry works in a bar in Borechester . . . this must be Harry's bar . . . what am I going to do? I consider bolting out through the door (risking getting spun around at high speed). But curiosity overcomes me, and I creep to the corner of the archway that leads into the bar area, and peep around it. It *is* Harry!

The manager is having stern words with Harry.

'You understand the importance of not contravening bar regulations? James is not meant to be here today. I am ultimately responsible for him while he is here – and I should have been informed. I am sending you home now, James, and I do not expect you back here until Monday.'

'Yes, Mr DeVille.'

'Your friends are here to see you, James. But I would like all of you to leave the bar area immediately. Where is the other young girl?'

'You mean Alex? She's over there!' Mark points in my direction. I freeze. 'Alex!' Mark calls. 'Alex!' (SHUT UP, MARK!!!)

**MR DE VILLE** Harry is craning his neck . . . he has seen me! (AAAAARGH!!! I am dead.)

'Hey! Alex!' Harry calls to me. 'Good to see you! Stop hiding!'

Unwillingly, I step forward. I hear Harry say to the others, 'She's incredibly shy and retiring, isn't she? Considering she's a famous artist . . .'

'Who are you talking about?' Mark asks.

'LET'S GO, PEOPLE!!!' Abby has obviously worked out who Harry is. She grabs Mark by the arm and practically drags him out of the bar area, followed by a puzzled-looking James and a reluctant Tracey (who keeps looking over her shoulder and smiling at Harry, who is scratching his head and looking dazed).

Abby leads the way and we all file out through the revolving door, in an orderly manner.

'The things I do for you, Alex!' Abby mutters to me when we are outside.

'Thanks, Abby! That was just a bit too close for comfort!'

The rest of the afternoon is uneventful, for which I am truly thankful. I help Mark check out some checked shirts. He eventually chooses one, which bears more than a passing resemblance to one which Dad has had for *years*.

Tracey buys a black Crazy Cow strap-top with 'WILD!' emblazoned across it in big silver letters. (I think this may be a reaction to having to wear those working clothes.)

'Oh, look – there's Clare!'

'Hi, Clare!' I call out to her. 'Haven't seen you for ages!' I give her a hug. 'Where's the handsome vet?'

'What handsome vet?'

'We think you're going out with a handsome vet! That's why we never see you! Are you going out with a handsome vet?'

Clare smiles wanly, and shakes her head.

'I'm going to the chemist and get some mouth ulcer pastilles,' she says. 'And some more shampoo. And flea spray.'

'You've got fleas?'

'I'm not sure.'

Mark and James back away.

'Oh, don't be so silly!' Abby says to them. 'So you've still got a sore mouth, and sore hands?'

'Yes. I'm really worried because the fish died. I might have caught something from it.'

'Clare, I don't think humans can get fish diseases.'

'Who knows?' says Clare gloomily. 'It takes seven years to train to be a vet. How am I supposed to find out in two weeks if all these things are potentially fatal?'

We all stare at her. She certainly doesn't look very well.

CLARE CERTAINLY DOESN'T LOOK VERY WELL...

'But why did you choose to work at the vet's?' Abby asks.

'Because I've always loved animals!' 'But Mum and Dad would never allow me to have a pet, in case it destroyed the carpet.'

'A fish wouldn't destroy the carpet,' James points out helpfully.

'Please don't mention fish!' Clare pleads. 'Anyway, I know now that I only like healthy animals.'

'I can see that would be a drawback, working at the vet's,' says Mark.

'I've got to go,' says Clare.

'Oh dear!' says Abby, after Clare has wandered sadly away. 'I don't think she's enjoying Work Experience.'

'That's a real shame. Work Experience is GREAT!' Mark enthuses.

'I think next week will be more interesting,' I say, trying

to sound positive. 'But I'm worried about Kaz's exhibition. She's invited my whole family to the private view next Wednesday evening, and they're ALL coming! Mega-embarrassing! Er . . . would you like to come along, Mark, to lend me support? Kaz said I could invite one guest. If I could invite the whole gang, I would – believe me!'

'That's OK,' says Abby. 'On Friday I made sixty-two folders, bringing my total to a hundred and nine. I think they get Work Experience people to do all the boring jobs *they* don't want to do! So all I want to do in the evenings is flop!'

'Me too!' Tracey agrees. 'I need REST. And I have all those papers to read. I'm sure I never got this tired at school.'

'Maybe that's because you were having more fun,' says James. 'Work Experience is so BORING! I clear tables. Then I clear tables. After that, I usually clear tables. And next week I get to *lay* tables! But I like Harry. He's an art student, and he works behind the bar to earn money. Harry's OK.'

'Harry was hot stuff!' Tracey comments, drooling slightly. 'Why are you looking at me like that, Alex?'

'I'm not!'

With relief, I see from my watch that it is time to meet Abby's mum and go home. It is definitely time to CHILL OUT.

'Just think of Fabulosa, partying away with all those famous people!' Abby sighs enviously.

'Yes,' says Tracey. 'All those famous singers, famous actors, famous models, famous ARTISTS . . .'

'And her dad,' I add.

## Sunday July 7th

**Second and Final Day of the weekend**

(**Note:** When I become Prime Minister – which is a job I am seriously considering, as I've been told I will need another job to supplement my income as an artist – I intend to introduce the two-day working week and the five-day weekend.)


Today I am woken up at midday by Mum's excited voice calling up the stairs to me, 'Alex, darling – Daisy and Diggory are here!'

Daisy and Diggory are down from Scotland and are going to stay with Mike, Diggory's best man at the wedding. The very best news is that they are going to look for a house near here! Diggory has just heard he's got a job as Chief Librarian. I am thrilled they won't be so far away. Daisy will even be able to start her teacher training course again! This is the happiest I've been for ages!

I leap out of bed (again!), and rush to the top of the stairs, still in my pyjamas.

'Daisy! I've missed you so much! Come and talk to me while I get dressed!'

Daisy sits on my bed while I crawl under it looking for a missing top and some trousers, and my mascara.

'Nothing changes!' Daisy comments. 'Except that you seem to have your own make-up now, instead of borrowing – or should I say *taking* – mine!'

'Rosie's a real pain!' I complain to Daisy. 'She keeps going off with my lipstick and squidging it.'

'Sounds familiar,' says Daisy. 'I seem to remember someone else, not a million miles away, doing that.'

I tell Daisy about Rosie taking Yellow Bunny to school, and what happened to Abby last week at St Bart's.

'Abby will make an excellent teacher one day,' says Daisy. 'You can tell her I said that.'

'I will.'

Then I tell Daisy about Kaz's studio – and about Harry.

'Hmmm,' says Daisy. 'You should tell him the truth, Alex. He'll like you better if you're honest. And if he doesn't, he's not worth knowing.'

'Honestly!' I exclaim. 'You and Abby are both the same. You say the same things – you're both teachers!'

'No, Alex. Abby's your friend. And I'm your big sister.'

'I know you are. And I just want you to stay here with me – forever!' I give Daisy a big hug.

'It's strange coming back,' says Daisy. 'It's as though I've never been away. Except that you and the boys and Rosie are all growing up. 'That reminds me, Alex – where's that Fifi CD you borrowed? I never had it back. Alex, I want it back!'

Nothing changes.

Mum calls us down to lunch. Diggory tells me that he

has a boy called Rodney doing his Work Experience at the library where Diggory works.

'Rodney's a real character! There's nothing he doesn't know about bookbinding!'

'Really?'

'It's a dying art, but Rodders is determined to revive it.'

'Rodders?'

'That's what he likes to be called. And he knows a lot about medieval history and manuscript illumination. You'd like him, Alex – he's interesting.'

(I'm sorry, Diggory. 'Rodders' sounds about as appealing as rancid yak's yogurt. Mind you, there is probably not a lot to choose between Mark and his computers, and 'Rodders' and

**YOU'D LIKE "RODDERS", ALEX!**

his illuminated bookbindings or whatever.)

Later I go to check for messages on my phone. There is one from Clare: 'Something wrong with my mouth. Lips swollen like a fish. Feel ill.'

I send a message back: 'Clare – pleeease stop this. U R not a fish. U R fine. Please cheer up.'

There are no more messages. I heave a sigh, and wrestle with my conscience. Should I invite Harry to the studio tomorrow or not? Abby and Daisy have both told me that

I need to tell him the truth and I know they're right. Tomorrow would be an opportunity to do this . . . So I send a message: 'Would U like 2 come 2 studio 2morrow am?'

Almost immediately I get a message back: 'Yes'.

It is not a particularly long or detailed message, but it makes me smile – I just can't help it. But then I hear Abby's voice inside my head, saying, 'Poor Mark . . .' I shake my head. No! I know what I'm doing! It'll be fine. It was fine on Friday when Harry came to the studio. It was slightly less fine on Saturday at the hotel, but I don't want to think about that. And it'll be fine tomorrow . . .

Too soon, it is time for Daisy and Diggory to leave. I hate saying goodbye to Daisy. What if things go wrong and I need her? But they won't go wrong. And my friends will be there for me anyway.

'Don't cry, Alex! Oh dear!' Daisy exclaims, giving me a hug. 'Cheer up! As soon as Diggory and I have found a new house and settled in, you can come and stay! Good luck with the rest of your Work Experience! I'll let you know how the house hunting goes! Thanks for lunch, Mum! Bye, Dad! See you soon, everyone!'

Daisy and Diggory squeeze into their little beetle car, and it farts and kangaroo-hops away down the road and around the corner. They are gone.

I find it hard to sleep tonight. Lying in bed, my eyes keep opening wide. Perhaps I am turning into an owl. I hoot

### PERHAPS I AM TURNING INTO AN OWL

quietly. I think I may be going mad. Artists do that. I wonder if a session of Indian Clapping Sounds would help me? I don't think it would make me feel any better about the lies I've told Harry – or seeing Harry behind Mark's back . . . Poor Mark . . .

## Monday July 8th

**Day One of Week Two**

**7.15 a.m.** I am not pleased when the alarm goes off. No leaping out of bed today. I am seriously short of sleep. But the thought of seeing Harry makes my heart leap, even if the rest of me is reluctant to move at all. A few moments later, I get a sinking sensation as reality dawns – I am going to have to tell Harry the truth, and I need to sort out my feelings about Mark. It is all too difficult, too confusing, too early . . .

**7.45 a.m.** Mark arrives, bright and early, and confronts me in the hall.

'Alex?'

'Yes, Mark? What is it? I'd better go, or I'll miss my train.'

'Why did that boy at the hotel think you were a famous artist?' (Mark has obviously been brooding about this all weekend.)

'Oh, I don't know! Perhaps he'd been at the booze behind the bar. How should I know? Does it matter?'

'OK, OK! Don't get in a stress! I just wondered.'

'I expect he just mistook me for someone else, that's all. Now I've really got to go.'

I feel awful for snapping at Mark. I know it's because I'm feeling guilty. Mark must be wondering what's got into me.

### At the station

'The next train due at Platform 2 will be for Borechester, Plumbury, Spurge, Fluxham and Gorbling Sands. This train . . .'

(Don't tell me: This train is running approximately three years, two months, two and a half weeks, six hours and forty-seven minutes late. This is due to unnecessary engineering works.)

'This train is running approximately six minutes – I repeat, six minutes – late.'

Oh, well. It could be worse.

### On the train

I search for Harry, but I can't find him. I am becoming seriously stressed. Suddenly my mobile bleeps.

The guard looks in my direction, but I shoot into the

corridor before he can say anything. The message reads:
'Got an early train so C U at studio early. Bringing my
work to show you. Harry.'

Early? HOW early? Now I am panicking even more.

'Looks like you've seen a ghost, love. Your hair's
standing on end. HARR HARR HARR!!!'

I stare fixedly in front of me, ignoring the guard.

'Huh!' he grumbles, stamping my ticket. 'Some people
got no sense of humour.'

**At the studio**

There is no sign of Harry. What A RELIEF!

'Would you photocopy these price lists for me while I'm
gone, Alex?' Kaz asks. 'Thanks! About two hundred
should be enough. You said that you might have a visit
from a friend today. Please remember what I said on

I WILL DO ORION'S
HAIR FOR HIM ...

Friday. If anything gets damaged or even moved from where it should be while I'm away, you will NOT get a good report from me, and there will be serious trouble.'

'I understand.' (I feel sick – too much responsibility.)

'Now, where's Orion? Doing his hair, I expect. It takes him ages!'

(*I* will do Orion's hair for him. I just want them to GO.)

Minutes after they have left, there is a knock on the studio door.

'I didn't want to make you jump this time,' says Harry, grinning.

'Oh!' I exclaim, jumping violently. 'Sorry – I didn't sleep much last night.'

'Why was that?'

'I think I was worried you wouldn't turn up.'

'But I told you I would!'

'Yes, but there was all that business at the hotel . . . you probably think I'm completely mad!'

'Don't worry about it! I liked your friends. I didn't know you knew James. He's doing Work Experience, so he must be younger than you, I suppose?'

'Er . . . would you like some yak's yogurt? I have a pet yak. I think you can see her from this window over here. Her name's Gloria.' (It is still too early in the morning for Complete Honesty, and I don't want to spoil things too soon. I expect Harry will leave as soon as he knows the truth.)

'Oh yes!' says Harry. 'I can see a creature – you mean that brown, hairy thing on legs?'

'Yes.'

'A pet yak! You're full of surprises, Alex!'

Harry wanders around, picking things up and examining them closely. He holds a painting up to the light and looks at it.

I remember what Kaz said about it being my responsibility to make sure that nothing was touched, damaged or moved while she was gone. I glance nervously at the CCTV camera scanning us from a corner.

'Harry, you probably shouldn't touch things . . .'

'But I thought you didn't mind.'

'It's my responsibility.'

'Your responsibility? Hey! This painting's a bit different – it's a portrait of a man and two children. I can't read the signature, but it doesn't look like Alex. Is it one of yours?'

'No,' I say, miserably. I point to a half-empty mug of decaffeinated coffee, which I made for Kaz on Friday afternoon when she got back from Indian Clapping. It is still sitting on the draining board by the sink, waiting to be washed up. '*That's* one of mine.'

But Harry hasn't heard. He is still staring at the portrait. 'Who's it of?' he asks. 'Who's the man?'

'That's J.'

'Who's J?'

'Kaz's husband.'

'Oh? Kaz – she's the cleaning lady, isn't she? So this is a

portrait of the cleaning lady's husband, and her children.'

'Hello?' says a deep voice. It is Robert, standing in the doorway of the studio. 'Who's this young man, Alex? I don't think he should be touching the paintings.'

'Er . . . this is Harry. He's studying art.'

'I can see he's studying it. Please put the painting down, Harry.'

Harry, looking surprised, puts the portrait down.

'Who's this, Alex?' he whispers to me, while Robert sits at the desk in the corner and switches on the computer. 'Is he your agent?'

I give a sickly grin. This is all going horribly wrong. WHY did Robert have to turn up?! I was just about to tell Harry everything . . . But now it is too late. Harry has already picked up his own art folder and walked over to Robert's desk with it.

'You must be Robert the Agent,' says Harry.

'I suppose I must be,' Robert replies, not taking his eyes

off the computer screen. 'This damn computer's playing up again. I keep telling Kaz she ought to trade it in for a better one. It's a dinosaur. Excruciatingly slow!' He bangs the top of the monitor with his hand. The computer makes a clunking sound.

'It might be better to get some proper advice from a computer expert,' Harry suggests. 'Rather than expecting the cleaning lady to sort it.'

'What?' Robert asks irritably, turning to look at Harry.

'Anyway,' Harry continues, while I search desperately for a cupboard big enough for me to hide in. 'When did you first notice Alex's extraordinary talent? How old *was* she when you first took her on to your books?'

'Alex? You mean the girl who's doing her Work Experience here?' They both turn and stare at me. I flash them a dazzling, foolish grin.

'Work Experience?' Harry repeats. 'So . . . this isn't Alex's studio?'

CHEEEEEEESE!

I FLASH THEM A DAZZLING FOOLISH GRIN

HARRY HATES ME!

'No,' says Robert. 'This is the studio of Karoline Wetherby-Trendle, the famous artist. And I'm not sure you should be here.'

'Alex . . . ?' says Harry.

'Yes, Harry?'

'You've been having me on. *Very* funny. I don't like liars.'

'Harry!'

Harry turns his back on me. 'Before I leave,' he says, 'would you have a quick look at my work, Robert?'

'No. Get out!'

'What's going on?' Kaz has arrived back unexpectedly. 'Robert? What's the matter? I left Orion at the workshop – he's clapping like there's no tomorrow. He's really into it and it's *so* good for him. But I felt guilty about leaving you to do all the work preparing for the exhibition, and about leaving Alex on her own again, so I came back. But can anyone explain what's happening here?'

'I'll try,' I say.

Harry hovers nearby, apparently in no hurry to leave. When I have finished a rather garbled explanation, Kaz gives me a long, hard Stern Employer Look.

'This is a serious matter, Alex,' she says.

(Oh dear. Goodbye, Work Experience. Goodbye, job prospects.)

'You pretended to be me?'

I nod, miserably. I feel numb.

'But *why*, Alex? I don't understand.'

'I . . . I don't know why I did it. I say stupid things when I'm nervous . . . It all got out of hand. I wanted to tell the truth. I'm so sorry . . .'

I am close to tears. Everyone is staring at me. Robert clears his throat. 'When I entered the room, the youth,' Robert indicates Harry, 'was handling one of your paintings.'

(*Thanks*, Robert! You know how to make a bad situation WORSE!)

Kaz looks ready to explode, but Harry suddenly says: 'Look, I don't want Alex to get into trouble. I don't know why she lied, but then I sort of made assumptions, and I *think* she tried to tell me the truth once or twice . . .' He looks at me, and I nod vigorously (I don't care how uncool I look!). 'But she still shouldn't have done it,' Harry continues. 'Anyway, she *did* try to stop me touching the paintings. And I wouldn't have damaged anything. I'm a student at Borechester Art College, and I think your work is BRILLIANT!' He says this with such enthusiasm that Kaz's expression softens.

'OK,' she says. 'Well – if you're sorry, Alex – I can't see that any serious damage has been done. But you shouldn't tell lies, and I will have to decide whether any of this goes on your report to the school. Mr Chubb's coming in tomorrow to find out how you're getting on.'

(Oh no.)

'I'm *really* sorry!' I repeat desperately. 'I'm sorry, Harry!' I say, turning to him.

Harry gives me a hard look. 'Perhaps we'll talk later,' he says coolly, and turns to Kaz. (Harry hates me! But not as much as I hate myself for being so STUPID!) 'Can I show you my work, Kaz?' Harry asks.

'Yes, of course,' Kaz replies, ignoring Robert's vaguely protesting noises. He is still battling with the computer.

Kaz looks at Harry's work, which is full of bold shapes and bright colours.

'This is really good!' she says. Harry beams, and I give him the thumbs up. 'Look at this, Robert!'

'Eh, what? Yes, that's good. Very good. Yes – I like that! A lot.'

(OK, Robert. Don't overdo it.) I am beginning to feel jealous. The only reaction I got from Robert was, 'Hmmm . . . Hmm . . . Hmm.'

'Tell you what, Harry – why don't you come along to the private view of my exhibition on Wednesday evening? I think Alex was going to invite you anyway, weren't you, Alex?'

Harry looks at me enquiringly.

'Er . . . er . . .' (AAAARGH!!! I've already invited Mark! But this is probably my last chance to make up with Harry . . .) 'Yes! Of course!' I hear myself saying. (Double AAAARGH!!! Never mind – I'll be ill that day . . .)

'And bring your work along with you, Harry. I might be able to introduce you to a few people.'

'Great!' Harry exclaims. 'Wednesday's my night off from bar work anyway, so it couldn't be better!'

My feelings towards Harry are becoming complicated. I really like him, but I am beginning to feel jealous . . . and why should I miss an opportunity to show MY work to a few people?! Perhaps I won't be ill.

'Oh – bother this computer!' Robert exclaims, thumping the top of the monitor with his fist.

'Listen, my dad could fix that for you,' I say. 'That's his business, fixing computers. And building them. He does upgrades, facelifts. Whatever you want, really. He

works from our home.' (I feel this is the very least I can do!)

'Thank you, Alex,' says Kaz. 'That would be *very* helpful. I'll certainly contact him. Robert, you could take Alex home today, and drop the computer off at her house at the same time, couldn't you? And no more lies, Alex, or I will have to talk to your parents as well.'

'No, really,' I bleat. 'That won't be necessary . . . I will NEVER do anything like this again. EVER! I promise!'

'I'd better get back to college,' says Harry. 'Thanks for looking at my work, and I'm really looking forward to the exhibition.'

'Good,' says Kaz. 'Come to the studio on Wednesday afternoon, and we'll all go together.'

(I don't really want to think about that . . .)


**Travelling home in Robert's car**
Robert has a red convertible sports car, and I find the journey home therapeutic – the roof down, the wind blowing through my spikes. (That gel I use is good stuff – my spikes can withstand even a roaring gale!)

Daniel and Seb are just arriving home from football practice after school when we reach the house, and I step out on to the pavement.

'I don't believe it!' Daniel mutters. 'Your so-called Work Experience seems to be all about riding around in limousines and flashy sports cars!'

MY SPIKES CAN WITHSTAND A ROARING GALE
( TOTALLY HEDGEHOG ! )

'Leave me alone, Daniel – I've had a hard day! Take this and give it to Dad.'

I hand my brothers various component parts of Kaz's computer, and Robert staggers in with the rest of it. I carry in the printer.

'Dad, this is Robert. He's Kaz's agent. Kaz's computer doesn't work.'

Dad shakes hands with Robert, and they discuss the computer. Mark stands beside them, listening and craning his neck to look at the computer (he has hardly looked at *me*. What have *I* done?! Or, to put it another way, what does he know?)

'Well,' says Dad. 'I think young Mark here can fix this, can't you, Mark?'

Mark nods vigorously. (Vigorous nodding is *so* uncool . . . but then I remember that I am not exactly the World's Coolest Teenager just at the moment, and I haven't been very fair to Mark.)

After Robert has left, Mark asks Dad if he can stay on to

help with Kaz's computer. Dad says that he can, just this once – as long as he phones his parents to make sure it's all right with them.

'You really are a great help to me, Mark!' says Dad.

Mark blushes. (He's so sweet! I want to hug him.)

'I'll be back in a moment,' says Dad, going out of the office.

While Dad is gone, I ask Mark why he is ignoring me.

Mark shrugs. 'Why do you always tell lies, Alex?'

'Wha . . . at? What lies?' (I am stalling . . . I don't know how much he knows.)

'Well, explain this: James called me just before you got back – and I don't appreciate getting calls while I'm at work, but your dad said it was OK, just this once – and James said that he and Harry had been talking this afternoon, because Harry saw him at the hotel. And apparently you and Harry *do* know each other. And Harry told James about you saying you were a famous artist, and pretending the studio was *your* studio, and . . .'

'Well, that wasn't very nice of them, was it? Talking behind people's backs and saying stuff about them is just as bad as telling lies!'

I am so upset that I am shaking. I would have preferred to tell Mark the truth myself, rather than have him find out from a third party. I HATE James! I don't *want* to hurt Mark! He is looking sad and reproachful . . .

'Talking about other people is what girls do all the time,' says Mark.

'That's different. That's girl talk.'

'Well, this was boy talk. I think it sucks that you lied to me.'

'I didn't! I just hadn't got around to telling you.'

'So you and Harry are going out, are you?'

'No.'

'You're lying again.'

'I'm NOT! Stop getting so stressed! I can explain . . .'

'Alex, I have work to do. Please stop harassing me.'

I throw my hands up in exasperation and storm out. I pass Dad on the stairs.

'It's fun having Mark here, isn't it, Alex? Do I detect an office romance going on?'

'Shut up, Dad!'


Sitting on my bed, still shaking, I decide to phone a friend, as I really need to talk to someone . . . (Preferably someone who likes me!)


**Phone call to Abby**

'Hello, Abby.'

 'Hi, Alex. How are things? You sound upset.'

 'I am. Harry knows everything. He hates me.'

 'I'm sure he doesn't . . .'

 'And Mark knows everything too. And *he* hates me!'

 'No, he DOESN'T!!!'

 'It was James who told Mark.'

 'Oh . . . I see. I'm sure he didn't mean to cause any trouble, Alex. James isn't like that!'

'I know he's your boyfriend, Abby, so I won't say anything. I know the whole thing was my fault in the first place. Please don't say, "I told you so"! I suppose it was bound to end in tears. My life's a mess. So much for being an artist. The only brush I get to use is the one I sweep floors with. I am so BORED! This is depressing. I want to think about other things. Have you made any more folders?'

'Yes, loads. I'm fed up with it. Sometimes I get to read with the children, but mostly I do boring stuff. I thought I was going to get teaching experience, but I'm getting folder-making experience instead.'

'How do you get on with the other teachers? Do you go in the staff room?'

'No, I feel weird going there. So I come home at lunchtime. Some of the staff are friendly – like Colin. But the others make me feel like I'm still at school.'

'You *are* still at school, Abby.'

'Yes, I know . . . I think I wish I was back there, with you and the rest of the gang. I had an e-mail from Tracey.'

'What did she say?'

'She's fed up! She spends her whole time making tea and coffee for everyone, and one of the lawyers – Mr Sneed, I think – keeps standing too close and breathing down her neck. She said she wanted to feed his tie into the paper shredder.'

'That sounds more like Tracey!'

Abby laughs. Things suddenly seem more normal.

Tracey has obviously not been instantly catapulted into a high-flying career, leaving the rest of us behind. This is a relief!

As I have nearly used up all the phone credit Mum gave me for emergency use, I say goodbye to Abby.

My phone bleeps. It is a message from Rowena: 'Work Experience is GREAT!!! Do not want to go back to school EVER!!! Scott bought me can of Coke!!! YUM!!!' (Does she mean Scott or the Coke?) 'Leisure centre full of weird people 2day, sitting in circle clapping! CU!'

Rowena sounds happy. Unlike Fabulosa, who has sent me an e-mail to say that her dad wouldn't let her go to a

THERE WERE ALL THESE
WEIRD PEOPLE...

## CLARE LOOKS PALE AND PUFFY
## (A BIT LIKE A PUFFER FISH)

celebrity party with a reporter from *Tarte* magazine, and that she keeps having arguments with her father, and now she wants to leave home so that she can have more freedom. I e-mail her back to say that parents can't help being annoying, but that she shouldn't rush into anything as drastic as leaving home. Later on I get another e-mail saying that she has made up with her dad, and that she is coming to Kaz's private view next Wednesday with her parents.

I also have an e-mail from Clare, saying that she is really worried that she has made the wrong choice for her Work Experience, and feels ill. I write back, telling her to take it easy. I ask her if she's thought of going to the doctor, and maybe talking to the school about Work Experience – I'm sure Mr Chubb would be sympathetic.

After I have sent the e-mail, I realise that I am exhausted. Sorting out my friends' problems has left me with no time to think about my own! This is probably a good thing.

I can hear Dad downstairs, persuading Mark to go home.

'You've done a brilliant job!' says Dad. 'Mrs Wetherby-

Trendle's computer is fine now. But you'll get me into trouble for working you too hard!'

'My mum and dad said it was OK. I don't mind staying on . . .'

'Well, I mind. Come on now, Mark – time to go! I'll drive you home because it's late.'

'OK . . . thanks!'

I hear the front door close. Mark didn't say goodbye. I experience a strange pang in the pit of my stomach. I don't want Mark to hate me. Or Harry. I didn't mean to hurt anyone.

I find it hard to sleep tonight. I have turned into an owl again. (Twit-twoo.) I think it is the fact that my life is a mess, coupled with the prospect of a visit from Mr Chubb to the studio tomorrow. What will Kaz say to him?

## Tuesday July 9th

### Day Two of Week Two

**7.45 a.m.** Mark and I say 'hello' to each other in an over-polite way. Then he disappears into Dad's office, closing the door behind him and shutting me out. I don't like this. I wonder whether to knock on the door and remind him that he's meant to wait in the kitchen until Dad is ready – and tell him that I'm sorry for everything – but my brothers choose this moment to come stampeding down the stairs – and I decide to leave for work instead.

'Tricky situation with Mark, isn't it?' Daniel calls after

me. (I don't believe it! Has Mark been talking to him?! Or has Daniel been eavesdropping again? I don't have time to find out.)

## At the station

I have *missed* the train! Can my life get any worse? The next train will get me to work forty-five minutes late! And I won't get to see Harry either. This is just GREAT. Late for work on the day that Mr Chubb visits the studio. WONDERFUL.

## Arriving at work, one hour late

(The next train was an additional fifteen minutes late – this was due to 'essential buffer maintenance', whatever that means.)

I am surprised to find Clare in Kaz's garden assisting the vet, who is attending to Gloria the yak. 'Did you remember the yak restraining irons, Miss Clark? And the hoof grapplers?'

'Yes, Mr Bulstrode.'

I have a brief chat with Clare, who says that my e-mail helped. She's going to see the doctor *and* to talk to Mr Chubb about Work Experience.

I creep up to the studio, hoping that Mr Chubb is not there yet and that Kaz will not notice me, so that I can pretend I've been there all the time.

'You're late!'

'Sorry, Mrs Wetherby-Trendle . . . er, I mean, Kaz.'

'Why are you late?'

'The train . . .'

'I don't want to know! This is not good enough. Especially after yesterday. But I am prepared to say nothing more about that whole incident as long as you promise *never* to do anything like that again.'

'Oh, I do! – I promise! Thank you! And your computer's fixed.'

'Oh, that's good news. I'll send Robert to pick it up. Please thank your dad for me, Alex, and ask him to send his invoice. Your father's a very clever man.'

'Well, actually, it was a friend of mine – Mark – who fixed it for you. Mark's doing his Work Experience with my dad, and he's brilliant at anything to do with computers.'

'Alex!' Kaz rushes over to me and starts feeling around my head with her hands – not actually touching my head, but very close. (Er, help!)

'Alex!' she exclaims again. 'When you said the name Mark, your aura positively flared!'

'Did it? Well, it's a bit awkward at the moment. We've sort of fallen out. I'm stressed, that's all.'

'But Alex, I am talking about the fire of love. It burns in you, Alex! It flares like dragon's breath and sends out fantastic crimson and gold tongues of fire and swirling sparks whenever you say the name Mark!!!'

(OK, so my aura's gone hyper. It's clearly out of control

MY AURA IS OUT OF CONTROL...

and doesn't know what it's doing. My aura is having a nervous breakdown, like the rest of me.)

'Where's Mr Chubb?' I ask, glancing around anxiously.

'He'll be here soon. He's got a lot of people to visit. Alex, would you sit on that stool and let me paint your aura, just as it is now? And if you could say the name Mark every sixty seconds, just to keep the fires burning . . .'

(Right. I just hope no one comes in . . .)

'OK. But I feel it might help me if I could do something constructive while I sit there,' I say to Kaz. 'If only to stop me going completely mad. So would you mind if I get a notebook and interview you? I'm supposed to interview you as part of my Work Experience.'

'OK, Alex. I'll answer your questions. But try not to move about too much – it blurs the colours of your aura. And the colours are splendid!'

Clutching my notebook and pencil, I perch on the stool in all my splendour and begin the interview.

*Me:* 'When did you first know you wanted to be an artist?'

*Kaz:* 'On the day I was born. Actually, before I was born. I remember admiring the rich colours inside my mother's womb.'

(This is getting weird. Let's move on.)

*Me:* 'OK. Next question. How did you get started?'

*Kaz:* 'I went to art college. Then I took my portfolio around as many galleries as I could, until I found one gallery that was interested. They put one of my paintings on their walls.'

*Me:* 'Were you always just an artist? Or did you have to get another job?'

*Kaz:* 'I did all sorts of things. I worked as a waitress. Alex, your aura is fading slightly. Could you remember to say "Mark", please?'

*Me:* 'Mark!'

*Kaz:* 'Thank you. That's much better. You're positively ablaze!'

*Me (moving on):* 'So when did you become a full-time artist?'

*Kaz:* 'I married the owner of the gallery. That helped.'

*Me:* 'You mean . . . ?'

*Kaz:* 'J Wetherby-Trendle. That's right. He was the owner of Wetherby-Trendle Fine Art.'

*Me:* 'And when did Robert become your agent?'

*Kaz:* 'The year Orion was born. Robert is Orion's godfather.'

*Me:* 'Do you think I should leave school now and become a full-time artist?'

*Kaz:* 'If you do that, you could end up with no qualifications, doing a dead-end job for the rest of your life.'

*Me:* 'So what should I do?'

*Kaz:* 'Stay on at school. Go to art college. Maybe get another job to help support yourself. Say "Mark".'

*Me:* 'Mark! Why don't you like my work?'

*Kaz:* 'What? Is that part of the interview?'

*Me:* 'Probably not. I just wondered.'

*Kaz:* 'Alex, I don't know what gave you the idea that I don't like your work! I *love* your work! Those cat drawings are beautiful. In fact, I'm intending to introduce you to a friend of mine on Wednesday evening. She loves cats – she has seven of her own – and she wants someone to paint their portraits. She'd pay you for it.'

*Me:* 'Oh – wow! Cool! I just hope I can do it well enough!'

*Kaz:* 'Of course you can. And I was wondering if you'd do a portrait of Gloria, our yak? She's having her hair cut today, so that she'll look her best.'

*Me:* 'Yes, I'll do a portrait of Gloria! I

ROBERT IS ORION'S GODFATHER...

could start my own pet portraits business!'

*Kaz:* 'Why not? But it might be a good idea to do business studies, so that you're sure you know what you're doing. You've got the flair – and the imagination – to start a really creative business. You just need sound business sense as well.'

*Me:* 'Or a rich husband. Sorry! That was meant to be a joke.'

*Kaz:* 'It's OK, Alex. I've finished sketching your aura. I can work on it later. Has the interview finished?'

*Me:* 'I think so.'


Mr Chubb arrives while I am cleaning brushes. Kaz greets him, and offers him tea (decaffeinated or herbal – Mr Chubb chooses decaffeinated). I grin (foolishly, no doubt) at Mr Chubb, and make myself busy with the kettle, straining my ears to overhear what they are saying about me.

'No, I have absolutely no complaints about Alex,' I hear Kaz say. 'She is polite, punctual . . .' (This is incredible, considering I was one hour LATE this morning!) '. . . tidy in her appearance . . .' (I am aware of Mr Chubb staring hard at my hair.) '. . . friendly and responsible, and willing to learn from her mistakes.'

'Mistakes?' queries Mr Chubb.

(Uh-oh. Here we go. I thought Kaz wouldn't mention yesterday . . .)

'She defrosted the fridge without being asked to, and all the yak's yogurt went off.'

'Ah,' said Mr Chubb. 'Alex can be a little impetuous, I've noticed. Our students have been warned not to touch machinery unless they are told to do so, so Alex should not have done that. She could have seriously contravened Health and Safety Regulations, by allowing dangerous bacteria to multiply in the yogurt.'

(Machinery? It was a FRIDGE.)

They both stare at me very seriously, and I have the urge to laugh hysterically.

'On the other hand,' Kaz continues (obviously feeling the need to lighten the mood), 'Alex showed initiative when she decided to defrost the fridge. She also arranged for my computer to be fixed, for which I am very grateful. Her attitude is positive and cheerful, and I have no serious criticism to make.'

I meet Kaz's eye and give her a huge smile – Kaz is a star! She could have landed me in serious trouble, but she has obviously decided to give me a chance. I won't let her down – and I won't let myself down either! No more lies!

'How do you feel you're getting on, Alex?' Mr Chubb asks.

'Oh, I'm really enjoying being here, Sir!' I reply. 'I've learned such a lot.'

'Such as?'

'Er . . . how to wash brushes, and . . . be responsible.'

'Good. That's very good. This certainly is a wonderful studio.'

Inwardly heaving a sigh of relief, I hand Mr Chubb his mug of tea and go back to washing brushes and rinsing jars. Mr Chubb is more interested in looking around the studio. I overhear him asking Kaz how much she would charge to paint a portrait of the Chubb family. He looks very taken aback when he hears the answer, and leaves soon afterwards, but not before congratulating me again on doing so well.

'And don't forget to thank Mrs Wetherby-Trendle before you leave,' he whispers to me. 'That's very important.'

'I won't forget, Mr Chubb.'

**Girls get-together (after work)**
Fabulosa, Tracey, Rowena, Abby, Clare and I are all gathered in my room, listening to music. (To my relief, Mark was not in the house when I got home. Dad said he was very tired and went home early.) I have just finished telling them about my idea for Pet Portraits.

'Do you think Mr Bulstrode would let me put up a notice at the vet's, advertising my services as a pet portraitist?' I ask Clare.

'I don't know. Maybe. Is that what you're going to do, instead of going back to school?'

'No. I'm going back to school. You're all going back, aren't you?' They all nod. 'Yes, I thought so. I'd miss you all too much if I left.'

'Zak may be leaving,' Tracey says. 'He loves working at

the estate agent, and they've offered him a full-time job with the chance of promotion. But he's only considering leaving because he's definitely got a job to go to. And it's a job he knows he enjoys.'

'It would be scary if you didn't have a job to go to,' Rowena remarks.

'How did you get on at the doctor's, Clare?' I ask.

'Oh, fine! He said he thought my symptoms were an hysterical reaction to doing a job I really don't enjoy. So Mr Bulstrode's going to phone Mr Chubb tomorrow, and I probably won't have to go back. Mr Bulstrode said he'd tell Mr Chubb that I worked really well, even if I didn't enjoy it.'

'That's nice.'

'How's your job going, Fabulosa?' Abby asks.

'I make loads of coffee, like Tracey. These magazine editors, they drink too much coffee. It's like, "Fabulosa! Fetch me a cappuccino!" and "Fabulosa! Get me an espresso!" If I'm lucky, I get to use the photocopier. That's as exciting as it gets. It is not glamorous. The Beauty editor has spots and facial hair.'

'What about your cousin – the Fashion editor?'

'She's fed up with working for *Tarte*. She's put in for a transfer to *Accountancy Weekly*!'

I am obviously not the only one to feel disappointed and disillusioned by my Work Experience. Being stuck at school is probably better than being stuck in a boring job, in a traffic jam, or on a train going nowhere, or in an office.

## THE BEAUTY EDITOR HAS SPOTS AND
## FACIAL HAIR

But there are still a few days to go – anything could happen. (Although I am deeply worried by the prospect of tomorrow evening with Harry and Mark BOTH at the private view, AND my family!!!)

'I think this Work Experience thing is getting us down!' I exclaim. 'Let's go back to school and have some fun!'

(I can't believe I just said that, but I actually mean it! I may have to lose the spiky hair and big earrings when I go back to school, but it will be worth it to be back with my friends, doing school stuff . . . I think I need more time to prepare for the Rest of My Life.)

Fabulosa and Abby stay behind after the others have left, and I voice my concerns about the Harry/Mark situation, and the prospect of both of them being at the private view.

'I could be ill, I suppose,' I say, 'and not go.'

'No!' exclaims Fabulosa. 'I want you to be there, Alex – I *need* you there. Peppi will let me go off on my own with you at the exhibition. If you are not there, I will have to stand by his side all evening, looking stupid!'

'You never look stupid, Fab! But OK, I'll go.'

'I'm feeling left out!' Abby says.

'I'll have a word with Kaz tomorrow. I'm *sure* she'd let you come, if you'd really like to. I'd feel better if you were there. I'll send you a message to say if it's OK, and Mum and Dad can bring you with them – I'll already be there. You won't be too tired from work to come, will you?'

'Of course not! I'd love to come,' says Abby. 'I'm . . . curious. And I'll be there to comfort you, Alex – if anything awful happens!'

'Now you're worrying me . . .'


After my friends have gone, I find Mum and Rosie in Mum's bedroom. Mum is trying on outfits for tomorrow night.

'What do you think, Alex?' she asks, posing in a lemon-yellow evening dress (she looks like a banana), with thin shoulder straps and a low-cut back. 'Would it be too much if I wore the fuchsia jacket with it?'

'It would be . . . too much. I prefer your black trousers and long black jacket. I think you should wear something that merges . . .'

'Merges? With what – the background?' Mum seems offended. Recovering, she carries on. 'I was thinking of dressing Seb and Henry in their pageboy costumes – it seems a shame not to make more use of them.'

'Yes!' squeaks Rosie. 'And I could wear my bridesmaid dress!'

'NO!' I exclaim. Then, taking a deep breath to calm myself. 'Couldn't you all just look . . . NORMAL? *Pleeease?!*'

The only member of my family, apart from myself, with any concept of looking cool is Daniel – I just hope I can dissuade him from wearing his 'Waspman' T-shirt, which is getting too small for him, but which he refuses to throw away.

## Wednesday July 10th

**Day Three of Week Two: Exhibition Day!**

**7.55 a.m.** No sign of Mark. He is late (for breakfast, if not for work). I think Kaz must have got it wrong when she said my aura was flaring every time I said Mark's name. It must have been flaring for some other reason – Harry, for instance? Harry doesn't whistle, or wear dreadful checked shirts like my dad, or talk about computers all the time. But since neither Harry or Mark likes me, what does it matter? (A sharp pang in my stomach reminds me that, unfortunately, it *does* matter to me.) I look in the hall mirror to see if my head is on fire, but I can't see anything apart from the usual spikes. (I wonder if I should carry a pocket fire extinguisher, in case I should flare too badly.)

## On the train

'Had a nasty fright, love? Your hair's standing on end! HARR HARR HARR!!!'

'Probably at the sight of you!' I retort.

The guard draws in his breath sharply, and wanders away, tut-tutting loudly and talking to other passengers about the rudeness of young people today. But I don't care, because I won't be seeing him again, as I have decided to take Dad up on his offer of a lift to work. I still want to be independent, of course, but I don't want to hurt Dad's feelings by refusing to let him drive me.

I am not sure if Harry will be on the train today or not. There is no sign of him. I feel a sense of relief, but I will have to face him this afternoon when he joins us at the studio to go to the exhibition. (And I do *want* to see him. Oh . . . I'm confused!)

## At the studio

At first I cannot see Kaz. Then I hear a rhythmic clapping and I find her sitting cross-legged on a mound of cushions at the far end of the studio, eyes closed, clapping. Robert is standing nearby, drinking a cup of coffee.

'Kaz is stressed, Alex,' says Robert. 'It's the strain of mounting this exhibition. I keep telling her she has nothing to worry about, but all her biorhythms have become de-synchronised. We're hoping that the clapping will help. In the meantime, she needs space.'

Robert jerks his head, indicating that I should get out.

(Space? There is more space in this studio than most people have in their entire houses! But I can take a hint.)

'I'll . . . I'll go and do a few preliminary sketches of Gloria,' I say. 'Kaz asked me to do that. So I'll go now.'

KAZ IS STRESSED

Fortunately, it is a fine, sunny day. I have borrowed a sketchbook and pencil from the studio, and I sit down on a grassy bank, at a safe distance from Gloria.

'Morning, Gloria!'

But Gloria is not in a co-operative mood. She turns her back on me.

'Eurgh! Gloria! Did you *have* to do that?!'

There are yakpats everywhere (like cowpats, only worse).

'Mind if I join you?' says a familiar voice.

'Harry!'

'You're early!' I say in surprise.

'Yes. College has finished for the summer, and there was nothing else to do. My dad was coming in to Plumbury today to do something, so he gave me a lift.'

(Couldn't he have offered me a lift? I can't help wondering – but I say nothing.)

'Kaz was in the studio, clapping,' Harry continues.

'I know. She's stressed.'

'Robert told me to get out. So here I am. That's a good drawing, but the horns need to be longer. Can I have a go?' (He seems to be ignoring everything that happened the other day. He can't have forgotten, but have I been forgiven?)

Harry takes the sketchbook and pencil and does a quick portrait of Gloria. It is very good.

'That's . . . very good,' I say. (I am repeating to myself: 'It is uncool to be jealous. It is uncool to be jealous. It is uncool to be jealous . . .')

'I'm really glad we met, Alex,' says Harry.

(I am no longer jealous. I have gone all gooey instead . . . and I should think my aura is visible from outer space.

'You mean you don't mind about the other day and all that stuff I said? I'm really sorry, you know, and I . . .'

Suddenly Harry kisses me. Just as he does this, Gloria lifts her tail and farts, making a noise like a trumpet. Harry and I fall about, helpless with laughter. Harry rolls down the bank and lands in an enormous yakpat.

'Oh, my God!' I shout. He is covered in it. 'Don't come near me!'

Harry chases after me, and I head back to the house, uttering girlie screams galore.

Kaz is in the conservatory with Robert. She has stopped clapping. 'Harry! Alex! Come here! We need help taking the few last paintings to the gallery. The clapping has worked like a charm – I am reborn!' Kaz raises her arms and takes a deep, cleansing breath. 'My god – what *is* that smell?' she exclaims.

'It's Harry,' I explain. 'He rolled in some yak poo.'

'Harry! That was hardly sensible. Fortunately, nothing can disturb me now. Robert, fetch Harry some of Orion's clothes to change into. Then we will go to the gallery.'

While Harry goes to change, I am bombarded by conflicting emotions. I feel as though I am floating! Harry

PHRRRRPP!!!

THANKYOU, GLORIA

loves me! I want to scream! But at the same time I am getting pang after pang in my stomach every time I think of Mark . . .


**Ten minutes later**

'Wow, Harry! You look . . .'

Words fail me. Harry is wearing bottle-green corduroy flares and a loose-fitting tie-dye shirt in vivid shades of pink and purple.

'Don't say anything. I feel like a complete prat!' Harry grumbles. 'That Orion guy is weird.'

'Ssh! Don't let Kaz hear you!' (But I have to admit that the new Lurve of My Life – possibly – does look . . . strange.)

Kaz rushes towards Harry with arms outstretched.

'Harry! What a transformation! *Much* better. The trousers are a little on the short side, perhaps . . .'

'Ankle swingers!' I giggle. Harry gives me a look.

'Now,' says Kaz, clapping her hands once (uh-oh – not more clapping!), 'to business, everyone! The gallery is just around the corner, so we can walk there, if we each take a painting.'

I am given the now completed painting of my flaring golden aura to carry. It is the size of a small door – not heavy, but awkward to hold *and* see where I am going!

'That's a beautiful painting!' Harry exclaims. 'Even better than that other one, which you said was *yours*, Alex.'

'OK, OK. I've said sorry! And I mean it – I AM sorry!'

'Come along now, you two!' Kaz barks. 'No one must disturb the good karma today.'

## At the gallery

It is a great relief when we reach Plumbury Fine Arts. I was terrified of dropping the painting!

Nigel Farquahar comes fluttering across the gallery to greet us.

'Kaz! You look resplendent, darling! Mwah! Mwah! 'And who is this young man?' Nigel enquires, looking at Harry.

HARRY IN ORION'S CLOTHES

'This is Harry,' Kaz says. 'Harry's studying art, and you MUST look at his work, Nigel. It really is quite exceptional. I'm glad you remembered to bring it with you, Harry dear.'

'Harry!' Nigel exclaims. 'Good to meet you. And how very . . . attractive you look in those clothes.'

Harry edges away slightly. 'Hello,' he says gruffly.

'Don't worry, Harry,' I whisper to him. 'Nigel likes you.'

'I know,' Harry whispers back. 'That's what worries me!'

'Hello,' says a voice, just behind us.

Harry looks around. 'Bianca!' he exclaims. 'Good to see

you! I didn't realise you were working here!'

'Obviously not.' Bianca puts her hand on her hip and gives Harry a sultry look. She is chewing gum, as usual. (What is going on?! Would someone tell me? But no one does.)

Nigel enthuses over Harry's work. 'Most remarkable! Very, very talented . . . and so young! I particularly like that one.' He points to an abstract painting in strong, bold colours, intersected by black lines. 'Reminiscent of Korski, in his early days. May I display it?'

(I hope he means the painting.)

Despite his reservations about Nigel, Harry looks delighted.

'Of course!' he says.

I am NOT jealous . . . Yes, I am! It is all a bit too much to bear. I thought that my career was really going to take off during this fortnight, but it is Harry who is getting the big break instead – and he wouldn't be getting it if it weren't for me inviting him to the studio. And all I get to do is sweep floors. To make matters worse, I don't know what's going on – Harry kissed me, but now he keeps smiling at Bianca.

After a while, Kaz goes back to her house to get changed. Nigel disappears as well. Harry and I stay at the gallery and I spend the rest of the afternoon arranging glasses to go with the organic champagne and freshly squeezed orange juice. (I would have enjoyed this if Harry hadn't spent the afternoon smiling at Bianca.)

**5.45 p.m.** Kaz returns with J, Orion and Aurelia.

'Kaz!' Nigel exclaims. 'You are a bird of paradise! Please, spread your wings!'

Kaz lifts her arms. She is wearing a tent-like golden kaftan with silver embroidery and huge sleeves. J, on the other hand, is wearing khaki shorts and a shirt made of rough sacking material (he obviously didn't want to upstage his wife). Briefly, I wonder what Dad would look like with a pony tail. It is an unsettling thought. Aurelia looks relatively normal, in a short black

AT THE PRIVATE VIEW

170

dress, and Orion is wearing purple corduroy flares and a lime-green tie-dye shirt.

'You and Orion sort of match,' I whisper to Harry.

'Don't I know it!' Harry replies with a sigh.

But everyone's attention is soon focused upon Nigel, who is wearing a shocking pink linen suit and a predominantly pink floral kipper tie. (He is obviously not worried about upstaging the artist.)

I WONDER WHAT DAD WOULD LOOK LIKE WITH A PONYTAIL...

'Nigel!' Kaz exclaims. 'How lovely!'

Nigel beams at everyone and beckons to the waiter to bring drinks (organic champagne all round – but guess who has to make do with freshly-squeezed orange juice?).

Harry (who is allowed champagne) drapes his arm around my shoulders. Glancing quickly at his face, I catch him winking at Bianca. This is all wrong! What if Mark arrives now and sees Harry with his arm around me? I try to move away . . . I wish Abby would get here! I'm even looking forward to seeing my family, although I hope they won't be *too* embarrassing.

A journalist and photographer from the *Plumbury Magazine* arrive, followed by a journalist and photographer from the *Plumbury Gazette* (a rival publication). They are followed in turn by a journalist and photographer from

*Tarte* magazine (I guess that Fabulosa had something to do with this).

Thankfully, Harry moves away and sidles up to a pretty female journalist. (I am going right off him, and I *wish* I hadn't let him kiss me! Oh, where *is* Abby?! And I want Daisy!!!)

The guests begin to arrive, and soon the gallery is full of people quaffing organic champagne and admiring the paintings. Apart from one very tall, thin man who refuses champagne and says in a loud voice, clearly audible above the murmur of other people's voices, 'I am afraid most of these paintings strike the *most* discordant note with me! This is *not* Wetherby-Trendle at her best!'

'Who's that?' I ask Robert. 'He's really rude!'

'Oh, that's Quentin Frogmore-Queasly,' Robert replies airily, helping himself to more champagne. 'He's an art critic.'

'Why does he bother coming, if the paintings *and* the champagne disagree with him?'

'That's his job, I suppose. Anyway, if Quentin Frogmore-Queasly comes to your exhibition, you *know* you've made it. It doesn't really matter what he says.'

QUENTIN FROGMORE-QUEASLY

'I see.' (I don't, really. The art world is strange . . . It seems a rather shallow place.)

Mark arrives! I get a PANG to end all pangs!!! Mark has spiked his hair! And he is wearing a denim shirt over a white T-shirt and a pair of dark blue jeans. He looks AMAZING!

I decide to be brave, so I walk over to him. 'Hello, Mark. You look . . . nice.'

'Thank you, Alex. So do you.' Mark gives me an odd sideways smile. Then his smile changes to a broad grin. He has noticed Harry. More to the point, he has noticed what Harry is wearing.

'Harry fell in a pile of yak crap,' I explain. 'He had to change into some of Orion's clothes.'

'His trousers are too short!' Mark exclaims triumphantly.

'I know . . .' Beside Harry, Mark looks positively handsome tonight. And he is a much nicer person. There is no competition. I don't know what I ever saw in Harry – I love Mark!!!

'How did you get here this evening?' I ask Mark, steering the subject away from Harry.

'I had a lift with Fabulosa and her parents.'

'Oh.'

'There they are – over there!'

Fabulosa is walking towards us with Mr and Mrs Curvetti. Mrs Curvetti is an elegant woman, considerably taller than her husband, with dark hair styled so that most of it is pulled back from her beautiful face while a few

THERE IS NO COMPETITION . . .

strands fall perfectly. She looks like a supermodel. (I think of Mum in her banana dress – it is not a good thought.)

'Ah!' exclaims Mr Curvetti, beaming. 'This is nice, is it not? Fabulosa, now you have the company of your boyfriend *and* your good friend, Alex . . .'

My stomach turns over, but then I remember that Mr Curvetti is even more of an expert at saying the Wrong Thing than Dad is!

'I think we will leave you three young people together to have fun! Perhaps you will look and find me a painting that I can buy tonight!'

'Yes, Peppi,' Fabulosa replies. 'We'll do that.'

'There's your mum and dad,' Mark says to me. 'And Daniel . . . Seb . . . the whole lot of them!'

(Uh-oh. I hardly dare look!)

'Oh – and there's Abby!'

(Thank goodness!!!)

Rosie rushes up and clings to me. (Thankfully, she is *not* wearing a bridesmaid's dress. No, she is wearing her fairy outfit, complete with wand.) Mr and Mrs Curvetti make a great fuss of Rosie.

Mum and Dad come to join us, and Fabulosa introduces them to her parents. Abby stands close to me. 'Everything OK?' she whispers.

'Yes, so far!' I whisper back.

Mum and Dad do a great deal of nodding and smiling, and Mum seems to have developed a nervous laugh, throwing back her head . . . (I think it is time to pretend I am not related to them. At least Mum took my advice and wore the black suit.) I notice my brothers are following Bianca around and pestering her for more vegetarian canapés from the tray she is carrying. She scowls at them. Daniel waves to me (he IS wearing his Waspman T-shirt!) and gives me the thumbs-up sign (because I am with Mark?).

But when I look round, Mark and Fabulosa have wandered off together to look at paintings, leaving me with Abby. My heart lurches uncomfortably. Abby squeezes my arm. 'Don't worry, Alex!' she whispers. 'They're just friends – nothing more. Mark loves YOU!'

'Are you OK, Alex?' It is Kaz. Your aura is quite subdued.'

Abby stares hard at my head, as if expecting to see something.

## BENJAMIN BUTTERLY-BREADKNAP

'I'm OK, really. Who's Harry talking to?' (Harry is talking to a pink-faced man in a suit and bow tie.).

'Oh, that's Benjamin Butterly-Breadknap, one of the best artist's agents in the business. Apart from Robert, of course. He might be able to help Harry.'

(What about ME?! I feel like wailing.)

I notice that Fabulosa has gone to join her mum and dad, and Mark is on his own again. (Good!)

Harry has his arm around Bianca, who has joined him and the pink-faced artist's agent. He gives her a quick kiss on the cheek.

'Eurgh! What a sleaze!' Abby says. She obviously does not like Harry. I experience a sharp twinge, but it is not so much jealousy as feeling that I must be STUPID for letting Harry kiss me! There *is* something *else* making me jealous . . . I can't really explain all this to Abby right now, although she seems to understand without the need for me to say anything. That's the nice thing about her – and Daisy is like that too.

'Excuse me, Kaz. I'm just going to talk to Mark . . . Are you coming, Abby?'

'Come back in a moment, won't you, Alex? Mary Middlesmith wants to talk to you – she wants you to draw her cats.'

'Oh! Yes, OK!' (At least I have been noticed for my ability to draw yaks and cats! But can I make a living out of it? Is there much demand for yak portraits? Perhaps I should move to Tibet . . .)

'Hi, Mark. That's a good painting, isn't it?' I say. 'You know it's of me?'

'No – is it?'

'Yes. It's my aura. And it's the way I feel whenever I think of you.'

'Er, excuse me!' says Abby. 'I think two's company and three's a crowd! I'll just go and talk to Fab. See you later!'

'Er . . . I don't know what to say, Alex,' says Mark. 'You mean you get all this stuff sort of exploding out of your head when you think of me?'

'Yes.'

'Wow! I . . . er, I like you too, Alex. By the way, Fabulosa's just bought this painting for her dad.'

'Cool.'

'You should have seen the wad of notes she pulled out of that dinky little bag she carries!'

Mark whistles. (I forgive him for the whistling, but I wish he'd stop going on about Fabulosa.)

The rest of the evening is fun. I don't care about Harry any more. It was a mistake, that's all. (But should I tell Mark that I kissed Harry? I don't know. I must ask Abby.)

Mary Middlesmith, the lady with the cats, asks me to come to her house soon to draw her cats. Her friend, who is standing nearby, listening to our conversation, says that she would like a portrait of her parrot.

'Er . . . you know I'm still at school?' I say a little nervously. 'I'm not a proper artist. Not yet.'

'Ah! But Kaz told us that you are brilliant at drawing animals, and whatever Kaz says is good enough for us, isn't it, Josephine?' Mary says. Josephine nods in agreement.

Harry rushes over to me, breathless with excitement. 'Alex! Guess what? Benjamin Butterly-Breadknap is going to look at my work! He's actually going to look at it! He *might* even be taking me on to his books! And Quentin Frogmore-Queasly hates me! Robert says that's a good sign!'

'I'm pleased for you, Harry. I really am.' (Even if you only think about yourself, and you're as shallow as the world you're about to become a part of.)

Bianca wanders over and drapes herself around Harry. I get the impression that she has had too many glasses of organic champagne. 'He's MINE!' she drawls, scowling at me. 'So keep your hands off him!'

'Alex doesn't want him!' snaps Abby angrily. (She and Fabulosa have just joined us.) I feel myself going hot all over. Mark looks uncomfortable, and I am afraid to meet his eye.

'Time to go, Alex!' Dad calls to me. For once, Dad has said the Right Thing at the Right Time! I turn to him gratefully, and go with my family and Abby to say thank you and goodbye to Kaz. I glance back over my shoulder at Mark. He is talking to Fabulosa . . . I have a massive TWINGE . . .

## Thursday July 11th

**Penultimate Day of Work Experience**

**7.45 a.m.** Mark arrives at our house.

'Hello, Mark!'

'Hello, Alex!'

We stand in the hall, avoiding each other's eyes.

'Well, I must be going,' I say.

'Yes, I must get to work,' says Mark.

(That was an awkward brief encounter. I don't know whether to tell Mark about the kiss. I don't want to go on feeling that I can't look him in the eye, or that I'm hiding something . . . But there is a time and a place for everything, as they say. In the hallway of our house at 7.45 a.m. didn't seem right. I want to talk to Abby first. She's coming over this evening.

**7.50 a.m.** I realise that I can't leave yet. I have to wait for Dad to get the car out, as he is driving me to work this morning. So I make lots of cheese and pickle sandwiches while Mark eats several bowls full of cornflakes. Neither of us speaks. The only sound is of Mark crunching cornflakes.

Dad puts his head round the kitchen door. 'Ready to go, Alex?'

'Yes, Dad.'

'I'll be back soon, Mark. Would you defragment the hard drive on Mr Harmsworth's computer – and update his RAM?'

'I've already done that,' Mark replies.

'Excellent! Er . . . perhaps you could do some Hoovering?' Dad suggests.

### At the studio

Kaz and Orion are in the studio doing some Indian Clapping Sounds together. This is more than I can stand, so I go into the garden to complete my drawing of Gloria.

'Morning, Gloria!' I say.

'MOOOOOOOOOOOOOOO!' says Gloria.

'Thank you, Gloria! That was very polite!'

'PHRRRRRRP!!!' (Oh well).

I work hard on my drawing, and I am happy with the end result. It has taken me several hours to complete. When I take it to the studio to show Kaz, I am pleased to find that the Indian Clapping Sounds session has finished. I am less pleased to find that, while I was in the garden,

Harry has been to the studio and delivered a large painting of a multi-coloured yak, divided up into sections by strong black lines. Looking down at my straightforward pencil sketch of Gloria, I experience a sinking sensation. I can't compete.

Kaz comes over and looks at my drawing.

'Hmmm,' she says, thoughtfully. (Oh no – not the 'Hmmms' again. I had enough of that from Robert.)

'You know, Alex,' she continues. 'I like Harry's yak very much. Very much indeed . . .'

(OK, OK! Don't rub it in!)

'. . . But I prefer yours.'

'You do?'

'Yes. Harry's picture is clever, and technically brilliant. But it has no soul. You, Alex, have captured the essence of a yak. Looking at your drawing, I feel that you really *understand* what it's like to be a yak.'

(I do?)

'You have become a yak.'

(I hope not!)

'So I would very much like to buy your drawing from you, have it framed and hang it on the wall.'

(In the loo, I expect. But I am very, *very* pleased.)

'Wow!' I exclaim. 'That's amazing! But you don't have to pay me.'

'Yes I do, Alex. Where's that business sense of yours?! I have enjoyed having you at my studio so much that I would love for you to come back and work here in the holidays, if you'd like to. I would pay you, of course.'

'Oh, yes! That would be great! I've been wanting a holiday job, and I can't think of anywhere I'd enjoy working more than here! And I've been thinking . . .' (Dare I ask? I realize that this is my opportunity to ask a question that's been on my mind . . .) 'Is there any chance of an apprenticeship?' I ask in a rush, gabbling slightly. "It'd . . . It'd be so amazing if you could pass on some of your knowledge and techniques and stuff to me – or is that asking too much?'

'I'll certainly give it some thought, Alex. You've got considerable talent, you know!' (I glow with pride.) 'But first,' Kaz continues, 'I am sending you back to school with the Employer's Report at the back of your Work Experience Logbook, saying that you have been polite, punctual, reliable and a pleasure to work with. I know you didn't mean to be late on those two occasions – it was the train's fault. And I'm sure you'll never pretend to be me again, will you? I'm sure you know it's better to be yourself, Alex. You're a lovely girl. So I am giving you an excellent report.'

(Mr Chubb will cry with happiness!)

**Back home, in my room, with Abby**

Abby has just told me that Mr Scribbling, the headmaster of St Bartholomew's Primary School, has given her an excellent Employer's Report. Even better, Mr Chubb is pleased because Toby and Henrietta Chubb, who both attend the school, have told him how brilliant 'Miss Abby' is.

It is my turn to tell Abby *my* good news! 'Kaz wants me to go back and work there in the holidays, AND she liked my yak!'

'That's great, Alex! I'm really pleased for you.'

'But she said I'd become a yak.'

'No, you haven't. You're still Alex.'

'There's something I want to ask you, Abby.'

'What's that?'

'Well . . .'

'What? What is it? . . . Out with it!'

'I kissed Harry. Harry kissed me. Anyway, we kissed.'

'Alex!'

'And then the yak farted. But it didn't mean anything.'

'What? The yak farting didn't mean anything?'

'No! I mean the kiss – kissing Harry didn't mean anything, because I know now that it's Mark I really love.'

Abby looks doubtful. 'What about when he whistles? Or talks about computers? Or dresses like your dad?'

'Oh . . . those are just . . . I don't know . . . Every relationship has problems. You just work through them together.'

'You mean you put tape over his mouth every time he starts whistling?'

'Something like that.'

'So what did you want to ask me?' Abby enquires.

'I wanted to ask . . . do you think I should tell Mark that I kissed Harry?'

'I think it's best to be honest.'

'So you think I should?'

'I think it's best to be honest. So tell him about the kiss, but then tell him it was a mistake, and you regret it, and . . . well, take it from there.'

'Hmmmmm . . .'

## Friday July 12th

**Final Day of Work Experience**

**7.45 a.m.** I am sitting on the hall stairs, waiting for Mark. I have decided tell Mark that I kissed Harry.

Mark arrives.

'Hello, Mark.'

'Hello, Alex!'

'Mark, I think you'd better sit down. I've got something to tell you.'

Mark sits on the stairs beside me, which would be nice,

if I wasn't feeling so worried about what I am about to tell him. What if he takes it really badly? What if I break his heart?

'Mark . . .'

'Yes, Alex?'

'When I was in Kaz's garden, Harry came and sat with me. And . . . and he kissed me.'

'Oh.'

We sit in silence on the stairs for several minutes.

'Please say something, Mark.'

'Well,' Mark replies, sounding subdued. 'I suppose that means we're quits.'

'What? Sorry – I don't understand . . .'

'Harry kissed you. I kissed Fabulosa.'

'WHAT?! No . . . No, you didn't! You're trying to make me jealous . . . aren't you, Mark? You don't *need* to! That kiss with Harry didn't mean anything. It was a mistake. I really . . .'

'You don't understand, Alex. I *did* kiss Fabulosa. It was for real.'

'You . . . You *did* kiss her? When?'

'We had a long talk the day she took me home from your place in her car. I went to her house for a while first – she invited me. It's an amazing place, like a palace, full of paintings and statues and things. We went for a walk in the garden. The garden's huge . . .'

'Mark, what happened?' I am aware of a huge, double surge of jealousy, firstly at the fact that Mark KISSED

Fabulosa (how DARE he?!!!?!!), and also that Fabulosa invited him to her house and she has never invited ME!

'Don't get the wrong idea! We only talked, most of the time,' Mark says. 'She was telling me that you're an artist . . .'

'I think you knew that.'

'Yes. But she knows that I like you, and so she was giving me this talk on how I could make you like me more. She said that I had to give up whistling, and that you didn't like my checked shirt, and that I shouldn't talk so much about computers. She said I needed to smarten up my image, and she suggested what I should do with my hair. Then she said that I didn't need to change anything about myself for *her*, because she likes me just the way I am. And then I kissed her.'

'But . . . But . . . *I* like you just the way you are, Mark! I really do! Just maybe not the shirt, that's all . . .' (I HATE Fabulosa!!!) 'But, was it . . . I mean, was it . . . It *was* just *one* kiss . . . w . . . was it?'

'Yes.'

'You don't sound very sure.'

'OK! It was just one kiss. I haven't asked *you* how many times you kissed that Harry bloke, or how *long* the kiss went on for . . . Anyway, I don't care. I expect Fabulosa would go out with me again if I asked her.'

'But . . . !!!'

'But I'm not going to. Because I want to be with you, Alex, if . . . if that's OK with you. I really like you, even if you kissed Harry. That's going to take some getting over,

186

but at least we're being honest with each other.'

Someone clears their throat at the top of the stairs. It is Dad, waiting for us to get out of the way so that he can come down.

'Time to go, Alex,' says Dad. (He's probably right.)

Struggling with some complicated feelings which I do not fully understand – except that I have an overwhelming urge to hit Fabulosa over the head with something heavy, and I am FURIOUS with Mark for kissing her – I say goodbye to Mark, rather stiffly, and go to work for the last time this fortnight.

## At the studio

Kaz spreads out the pages of the *Plumbury Gazette* for me to see. (The *Plumbury Magazine* does not come out until the end of the week

I HAVE AN URGE TO HIT FABULOSA OVER THE HEAD ...

and *Tarte* magazine does not come out until the end of the month.) There is a full-page feature on the exhibition with pictures of Kaz and Robert and Nigel and Quentin Frogmore-Queasly, with Harry standing beside him. There is also a photo of Fabulosa, standing beside the painting of my aura.

'You know your friend Fabulosa's father bought the painting of your aura?'

'Yes.'

'I told her that it was you in the painting, and that your aura shines when you think of Mark.'

'Oh . . .'

'She said she wasn't surprised, because she knows how much you love him.'

'She said that?'

'Alex, I am sorry to have to tell you this, but your aura keeps turning green whenever you think of Fabulosa.'

(I feel my face turning red . . .)

'But, Alex, listen – you have *nothing* to worry about. I was watching Mark last night. He had the most beautiful golden aura whenever he looked at you, and *only* when he looked at you. It disappeared when he looked at Fabulosa. Well, it may have glowed very slightly when he looked at her, but hardly at all. It was nothing compared to the magnificent blaze when he looked at you.'

I can't help smiling.

'There! You look happy now – that's better! Your aura is flaring again!'

### Back home

That's it! Work Experience is over. It's back to the School Experience on Monday – and I'm looking forward to it! I want to be with my friends. The world can wait.

Dad tells me that he has given Mark an excellent report, *and* offered him holiday work and a possible apprenticeship. I don't mind . . . I will be working at Kaz's studio! I enjoy being with Mark more when we have a break from each other's company.

'But . . .' Dad adds, '. . . I'm not sorry to have a break from young Mark. That whistling was beginning to get to me.'

THAT WHISTLING WAS BEGINNING TO GET TO ME!

Tracey phones to say that she is *soooooooooo* relieved to get away from Hogsbreath, Whittle and Sneed (especially Sneed), and that Mr Hogsbreath criticised her for being two minutes late one morning, and for using her mobile at work. Rowena sends a message to say that the supervisor at the leisure centre has said that he is very pleased with her. Clare sends a message to say that her rash has now disappeared completely. Abby phones to ask if I'd like to go round to her place. And Fabulosa sends a message which says: 'I am so sorry – I kissed Mark. It was a mistake. I know he loves only you, Alex. Forgive me. Can we be friends, please?'

I sit on my bed, staring at the message from Fabulosa. As I'm sitting there, my phone bleeps and vibrates in my hand, making me jump. I have another message. It is from Mark. It says: 'I love U. And the new Pentium Processor XP3 Excel is amazing! I love it not quite as much as I love you.'

I send a message back to Fabulosa: 'Yes – we are friends! C U soon.'

## At Abby's house

Lying on Abby's bed, listening to music, telling Abby all about Mark and Fabulosa and how I've been honest with Mark and he's been honest with me ('Now you can go forward!' Abby comments), and that the prospect of going back to school on Monday, the world seems a more 'normal' place . . .

'Do you still want to be an artist?' Abby asks.

'No. I want to herd yaks in Tibet.'

'Seriously . . .'

'Seriously, I still want to be an artist. Which is why I'm happy to go back to school, because I don't feel ready to be *that* serious yet. At school you can make a mistake and someone will help you get it right next time. At work it's more final somehow. More serious. You could lose your job – it's scary.'

'I feel the same,' says Abby. 'I really want to be a teacher, but I want to take my time and do it properly, so that I get all the training and qualifications I need.'

'You need training, qualifications – and a Mars bar,' I remark.

'Why a Mars bar?'

'"A Mars a day helps you work, rest and play"!'

'Alex . . .'

'Yes, Abby?'

'You're mad!'

'Yes, I know! I'm an artist!'

When Abby has gone, I stroke the cat and reflect that cats have got it all worked out. No Work Experience for them! All they want is plenty of Eating Experience, Sleeping Experience, and an occasional bout of Going Completely Mad and Climbing the Curtains Experience. I wish I was a cat . . . On the other hand, they have to eat *cat* food, and go to the vet's. Nothing in life is perfect. Mark whistles, and my biggest break as an artist so far is having my ability to draw cats and yaks recognised (I have

CATS HAVE GOT IT ALL
WORKED OUT

become a yak!). I now know that my chances of being discovered by a wealthy American art collector are slim, and I think I will settle with going back to school in the meantime . . .

I'm not thrilled at the idea of 'becoming a yak', so I decide to become a cat instead. I shall eat, I may decide to climb the curtains (or maybe not), and then I shall SLEEEEEEP.

ZzZZZZZZZZZZZZZZZZZZ